KILLERS AT SEA

KILLERS AT SEA

ALAN JOSEPH

CUTTING EDGE

ISBN-13: 978-1-957868-02-8

Published by
Cutting Edge Books
PO Box 8212
Calabasas, CA 91372
www.cuttingedgebooks.com

CHAPTER ONE

The old man on the beach was dead. Logan put a hand against his cheek. Dry, wrinkled parchment, but warm. He'd been brutally beaten to death. Recently. His eyes shifted from the man's body across the sandy dunes. It was dawn and the surf thundered. Logan had known the old man for years. This morning, as he'd done every time he came to Kingdom Point, he'd come for clams, the big quahogs of the Carolina coast. If the old man had a name, Logan had never heard it. The "old man of the beach" was all anyone ever called him. A harmless, gentle old man. Now he was dead, slain in the soft, gray mist of the early morning.

The knot in Logan's stomach was cold anger, disgust, old pain brought to life. Logan's long, lined face was impassive as he started to go through the old man's pockets. Suddenly, a shot exploded, sending the sea birds screeching, and ripped into his sleeve. Only his eyes changed, blazed. With lightning-fast reaction, he moved. A sand dune to his right beckoned, topped by a thin line of tough railroad vines. He had just rolled behind it when another shot split the air, grazing his ankle as he rolled. He winced at the sharp, searing pain of it and flattened himself down into the sand behind the low dune. Edging upward, he peered out through the vines. Across a dip in the sand, behind the vines of another dune, he glimpsed long, blond hair—the real kind of blond, made yellower by the sun.

"Hold it!" Logan called out. "Listen to me."

The third shot thudded into the dune, showering him with sand.

1

"Bastard! Stinkin', rotten bastard. I'll kill you," he heard the girl say, words more sobbed than shouted. Another shot whizzed over his head. Keeping down, he called out again.

"Listen, you're making a mistake," he yelled. Another shot whopped into the sand. He rolled over and glanced around. A line of yaupon grew on the other side of the dune, starting left and wandering to circle behind the dune where the girl sat. Staying low, he pulled off his shirt and laid it against the dune-top vines. Almost at once, she fired again. Logan saw the bullet go through the shirtsleeve. He crawled down into the dune and worked his way to the yaupon, crouching behind it. Damnit to hell, he cursed, silently. He'd come to Kingdom Point to see Jennifer, to renew an old moment of peace and quiet. Instead, he was being used as a shooting gallery target by a babe with long blond hair. He crawled alongside the yaupon till he was almost opposite the other dune. He could see her better. He moved on, staying flat on his stomach, moving slowly so as not to disturb the bushes. The girl was intent on the dune where he'd been. Then, suddenly, he heard her voice.

"Why'd you have to kill him?" Logan heard. "I'll get you for that, I swear. You'll have to come out. I'll wait."

There was a choked sob in each word, as though it were torn out from inside her. But now he had circled around behind her and saw that she lay flat on her stomach with the rifle resting on the edge of the sand dune. Her legs were spread apart, her rear a round, full mound, inviting in the tightness of her jeans. He wanted to go up and pat it. But he knew that would get him killed. The girl was near hysteria. As he watched, she fired two more shots off, each shot a kind of curse, accompanied by a deep, choking sob. Logan stood up carefully, lifting himself first to a crouch, then rising to his full height. Moving with the silent grace of a jungle cat, he stepped forward carefully. The girl lay about twenty feet away. He'd crossed a little more than half the distance when she turned. She hadn't heard him, he was sure.

As she whirled, he saw blue eyes blazing and large breasts barely contained by her red-checkered shirt. She rolled on her back and swung the rifle over to fire as he twisted and dived forward. The shot exploded, and he felt the bullet tear past his ribs, grazing his skin. Then he was on top of her, grabbing for the rifle with both hands. He got a trip on the barrel and twisted, but she went with it, clinging to it like a squid to a lobster. He felt the movement of her knee and twisted his body to one side, just in time. She had brought her leg up sharply, trying for his groin.

"Bastard!" she gasped through clenched teeth. She let go with one hand and raked her nails across his face. Logan turned his head away and felt her hands grip his hair and yank. He brought one arm around, letting go of the rifle for a brief instant, and clipped her on the side of her jaw. She went limp, and he seized the rifle again and yanked it out of her hand. As he rose, she half-rolled over and then kicked out, sharply. The blow caught his thigh as he twisted away. He grabbed her leg, twisted and flipped her over on her stomach. She gasped in pain. With one big hand he pressed her face down into the sand and held her there, giving her just enough air to manage a few deep breaths.

"Goddamned little hellcat," he said. "Stop that and listen to me." She tried a backward kick, bringing her leg up sharply. It raked him across the side of his ribs. Tossing away the rifle, he brought his hand down with all his might across her tight, full little ass. She yelled. Yanking her by a handful of her long, blond hair, he pulled her up and tossed her down onto the sand on her back. The sand flew up as she hit, and she lay there, trying to catch her breath.

"I didn't kill the old man, damn it," Logan shouted at her. She lay there, chest heaving, her breasts drawing the red check of her shirt taut with each breath. Her hips, in the tight jeans, were narrow and flowed into long legs. Her lips were full, softly formed, with the lower one thrust out in a half-pout. Her sea-blue eyes glowered at him. She lay there for a long moment as her breath returned, and he stared at her, waiting for her to say something. Then he saw her hands, tensing, pressing into the sand. Another man might have missed it, but not Logan. He'd learned, once, to look for the little things and not forget the things you learned the hard way. When she flung herself up and over, rolling toward the rifle in the sand, he stuck out a foot and caught her in the belly with it, lifting her up and flinging her backward. She doubled up on the sand, hands clutched to her belly and her long blond hair falling down, partially hiding the pain on her face.

"Sonofabitch!" she gasped.

"I told you I didn't kill him," Logan said quietly. He took her by the shoulder and felt the softness of her flesh. Christ, he needed a woman. Even now, with this furious spitfire, he could feel the need. He kept his hand on the girl's shoulder, pressing her back into the sand, pulling her body straight. He knew his big frame almost blotted the sky from her view, and his hand on her shoulder pressed in with the hint of what it could do. But there was no fear in her blazing eyes—only fury.

"I'll tell you once more," he said, his voice menacingly low. "I didn't kill the old man. I came along and found him there."

"You were going through his pockets," she hissed.

"Yes, to find something with his name on it," Logan answered. He let go of her shoulder and stood up. He gazed down at her, thinking how beautifully wild she was.

"I came for some clams," Logan said. "I always do when I stop here at Kingdom Point. Why would I want to kill him?"

The question brought back a flood of pain, and he saw her eyes overflow at once. She got up on one elbow and looked across the spot where the crumpled figure lay behind a rise in the sand.

"Why? Damn, I don't know why," she sobbed. "Why should anyone have to kill him? He never hurt anybody. He never did anything to anyone. He was kind and good."

Logan didn't answer. Her questions were the same as his. He hadn't had any answers then, and he hadn't any now. Only to say that people killed people and right had damned little to do with it. He held out his hand. The girl took it, and he pulled her to her feet. He remembered once hearing that the old man had a girl who lived with him, a niece.

"You the niece?" he asked, crisply. She nodded and wiped her eyes with the back of her hand.

"You can get your rifle now," he said, and she looked up at him, frowning. "Go ahead," he said. "That ought to prove to you I didn't kill him." Her eyes still regarded him distrustfully. "If I killed him why don't I just shut you up, too?" he asked. "Go on, get the rifle. Maybe then you'll believe me."

It was a calculated risk. The girl walked over to the rifle and picked it up. Logan stood watching her and saw the cold hatred go out of her eyes.

"All right, I guess I believe you," she said. She came toward him, and he watched the slow, easy grace of her walk. She was as sensuous as the sea itself, as inviting, as invigorating, and as dangerous.

"What were you doing out here with the rifle?" he asked.

"I got up later than Pops and came out to help him," she answered. "When I found him I ran back to the house, got the rifle and ran all the way back here."

"And saw me beside him starting to go through his pockets," Logan finished. "And you just started shooting."

The girl's eyes on him were steady, her lower lip pushed out a fraction farther. "I guess I just didn't think or care about anything except killing somebody for what happened to Pops," she said. "Who are you, anyway?"

"Logan," he said flatly. "And I just stopped at Kingdom Point to see an old friend. I'm anchored off shore."

She swung around and let her eyes move out across the beach to the rolling surf, now blue and sparkling in the morning sun. The *Sea Urchin* was anchored a few hundred yards below where they stood and about a hundred yards off shore.

"That funny old beat-up one that dropped anchor last night?" she asked, turning to him. Logan was used to the *Sea Urchin* being called that. It was fine with him. He purposely let her peeling, chipped paint hide the powerful, seagoing hull and interior of hand-rubbed Burma teak, Philippine mahogany hull with keel and frames of Yacal and silicon bronze fastenings. The *Urchin*, like her master, preferred to wear old clothes. She could show what she had when it was necessary. That was enough.

"Yes," Logan answered. He saw her take in the powerful muscles of his chest, the width of his shoulders and the rippling movement of his back as he retrieved his shirt. "What's your name?"

"Julie," she said, her voice quiet.

"All right, Julie, I'll take you back," he said. "You can't do anything here. We can call the police."

"The cops!" she sneered, falling into step beside him. "That's a laugh. The only cops here are Chief Redmond and that big ape assistant of his, Luther. They won't do nothin'. Chief Redmond will say some of the rich kids from the other side of the point did it for kicks and that'll be the end of it. Luther will use it as an excuse to come out here to question me with more than his tongue hangin' out."

Logan was surprised at her bitterness. She walked away from the beach and back up across the small hillocks. Cresting the rise, Logan saw the house. It was like some bad joke, a caricature of all old houses ever built. Gray wood, unpainted, weathered, upper floors boarded, it sagged and leaned in all directions at once. There were crumbling towers at the front of the house, one at each end, and a widow's walk circled the roof line, bordering sagging gables. The front door was open, and they walked in through a foyer with dark flowered wallpaper and two sturdy, old chairs. The foyer opened up into a huge living room, cluttered with furniture that was more bits and pieces than whole. A stone fireplace took up most of one wall, and a dark-green, worn sofa filled the space in front of it. On a round table a hurricane lamp stood next to a welter of books. The corners of the room were crammed with oars, crab nets and heavy, wooden clam tubs. A roll-top desk nudged a jumble of boxes and crates at one side, and four heavy, stuffed chairs with faded fabric, were scattered aimlessly around the room. At the far end, a wall of windows stood open. The window sills were lined with cages that looked out toward the sea. A ringed plover occupied one cage, a tern another and a gull a third. Two field mice chattered in a fourth cage. Near the windows was an easel with a canvas on it, and a paint box leaning against it. The room spoke of people who had lived good lives of work, weather and contentment. As Logan watched, the girl walked around the room.

"He taught me so much," she said. "He knew so much. He knew why a particular kind of sponge is the way it is, why the sea birds fly differently when a storm nears, why the ocean and the land constantly borrow life from each other. He taught me to be aware of everything, to wonder at all living things."

She opened the center cage and took out a tern, stroking the feathers. Her lustiness was gone. She was all gentleness and sensitivity.

"He brought this one in with a broken wing and nursed it," she said. "He was going to let it go today."

Released, the tern flew out the window. It circled, wheeled and flew out to sea. Julie turned to the big man, her eyes boring into his. She was once again all earthiness, as though she'd tossed aside the cape she'd worn for a brief moment. She walked to the easel and took down the canvas.

"Who did the painting?" Logan asked.

"He did," she said, her voice small. "He used to like to paint the gray days especially, to find beauty in the things everybody else finds dull and boring."

She turned, anger in her eyes.

"But he wasn't one of those gabby old men, understand?" she said. "He wasn't full of empty words and armchair philosophy. He lived this way because he wanted to. He didn't make excuses and hide behind big words."

"And you?" Logan asked.

"I wouldn't have changed it for anything," she said.

"Not even the loneliness?"

She shrugged. "Loneliness is more inside than outside," she said. As she crossed the room, dismissing the conversation, Logan saw the scuba diving gear half hidden behind the edge of the clam tubs. She moved one of the air tanks, setting it up against the wall.

"Your equipment?" he asked and she nodded.

"I started diving when I was fourteen," she said. "I got interested in it. You could say it's a hobby, I guess. I like it under the water. It's another world. It's like eavesdropping."

Logan smiled. She certainly was unpretentious.

"Why'd you come here to Kingdom Point?" she asked, looking at him sideways.

"Seeing an old friend," Logan replied.

"A girl?"

He nodded. "But not the way you make it sound. She's just an old friend, someone out of the past. I stop to see her whenever I pass this way."

"Who is she?" Julie asked suddenly, bluntly. He was going to tell her it was none of her damned business, but he didn't. That was a mistake, but he suddenly felt sorry for her, for the lost look behind the defiance in her eyes.

"Jennifer Holden," he said and saw surprise flood her face.

"Jennifer Holden, the town librarian?" she asked. He nodded. He'd called Jennifer when he dropped anchor last night, just long enough to tell her he'd be there with clams for lunch. He remembered how wonderfully sweet her voice had sounded, with the bittersweet pain of the past in it. Not that he and

Jennifer had ever been more than friends. But she was still a part of that time and that pain. She was the only one he ever saw any longer, and he often wondered why. Perhaps there was a communication of the wounded between them. Logan brought his mind back to the blond creature watching him, and gave her a small smile.

"Where's your phone, Julie?" he asked. "I'll call the police for you."

"I told you they won't do anything," she said bitterly.

"They can take in the body," Logan said. "Where's the phone?"

"No phone," she snapped. "I'll go into town and tell them. You come, too."

"No, you don't need me," Logan said. "There's nothing more I can do."

"You could help me find who killed Pops," Julie said, glowering up at him. "I'm going to find them, whoever they are."

"Sorry, this is where I get off," Logan said.

"In such a hurry to get to Jennifer Holden?" Julie sneered. "She must have somethin' I didn't notice."

Logan's dark, probing eyes narrowed. "Watch it, doll," he said, a hard note in his voice. She was glowering, sullen with a defiant sexuality. "There's nothing more I could do. Sorry about the old man, really I am."

"You could stay here," she said. "There's plenty of room. You could help me find who killed Pops." She was suddenly all little girl, pleading, anxious. She could change moods like a chameleon changed colors.

"No dice, Julie," Logan said. "Sorry." He turned and started for the door.

"Sorry, my ass," she called to him. "You don't care a goddamned bit." He paused and looked back at her blazing eyes.

"I care, but I'll care alone, in my own way," he said. "And I don't expect you to understand."

"Jennifer will be glad to see you," the girl said. Once more, Logan paused, his big frame filling the doorway.

"Why do you say that?" he asked quietly, frowning at her. She shrugged, a lost, helpless little shrug.

"*I* would be," she murmured, hardly loud enough for him to hear, and his eyes narrowed as he looked at her.

"Thanks," he said, and walked out the door.

"Bastard!" he heard her shout after him. "Don't come back, hear?"

Logan grinned. He didn't intend to. He'd come to Kingdom Point to see Jennifer and the boy. He wasn't getting involved in a murder. It was lousy. It was stinking. But it was done, and he'd have none of it. He and the *Sea Urchin* had other places to go and other things to do. They had their own search, and he knew he could never explain it to Julie. He let thoughts of Jennifer elbow the girl with the long blond hair from his mind. Jennifer would understand his not staying. He started across the soft ground, half sand, when he heard a voice, cold, rough, commanding.

"Hold it," the voice said. "Turn around and go back inside."

Logan saw three men approaching from the right side, just cresting a rise in the ground. One, wearing a cream-color jacket and an ascot, held a snub-nosed .38. The other two, in sport shirts, had the flattened noses and rolling gaits of ex-pugs.

"Sorry, I'm on my way out," Logan said quietly. He started to walk on.

"Take one more step, and you sure will be," the cream jacket said quickly. Ha waved the gun. "Maybe you didn't see this?"

"I saw," Logan commented flatly. He calculated the distance and the odds. They were both bad, and he shrugged and turned back to the house. The three men followed him. Julie turned in surprise as he entered. Her eyes flicked to the three men behind him. Cream jacket stayed close to Logan while the other two fanned out into the room.

"Friends of yours?" Logan asked the girl, but he knew the answer. He shot a glance at the jacketed man. He was the type to get overconfident. Sooner or later he'd put the gun in his pocket. Sooner or later he'd make a mistake. Logan moved to the round table, his hand beside the hurricane lamp. "Look, I don't know what this is all about," he said, putting a note of fear in his voice. "I just want to get back to my boat."

"Shut up," Cream jacket snapped. He focused on Julie and leered as he took in her beauty. "Where'd the old guy put it?" he asked. "We don't have time to play around, baby."

"*You're* the ones who killed him," Julie snarled.

"I don't know what you're talking about." The speaker's glance swept to Logan, then back again to Julie. "One of you better start talking," he said.

"I came here to buy some clams," Logan said. He looked at Julie and saw something leap into her eyes, a glint of triumph.

"Fat chance," she said quickly. Logan's lips tightened. She'd seen the chance to draw him in deeper and had seized it with shrewish glee. Cream jacket's eyes were boring into him, and the man spoke to the others without moving his head. "Watch the girl," he said, and started toward Logan. That was when he made his mistake. Logan watched him drop the gun into his jacket pocket, easy confidence in his face. Logan seemed to be fearful as the tall man approached. Behind him, his hand closed around the brass base of the hurricane lamp. When the man moved within range, Logan smashed the hurricane lamp into his face, bringing it up and around in a hard, fast movement. The glass shattered and the man's face erupted in a dozen separate gushers of red as he screamed in pain. Logan raked the jagged slivers of the lamp back across the already sliced flesh of the face before him, now a dripping mass of red.

"Oh, my God!" the man said as he fell to his knees. Logan raked the side of his neck once more with the broken glass as the man's form fell beside him. "Oh, my God," he screamed as he rolled back and forth on the floor, both hands up to his face. The other two, frozen for a moment at the unexpectedness and savageness of it, gathered themselves and rushed at the big man. Logan flung the remains of the hurricane lamp at the nearest one. He ducked away, but before he straightened up, Logan smashed a looping right to his jaw, and he went crashing backward to the floor. The second one tried a tackle. Logan stepped back and met the man's jaw with his upraised knee. He heard the lower teeth being driven into the upper underside of the mouth and the figure dropped to the floor at his feet. The other one had recovered. As the man rose, Julie dived for the rifle she had stood in the corner. The ex-pug slammed into her waist with a thick arm, driving the breath from her and flinging her back onto the sofa. Logan tried a long-distance right, but he knew he was out of range, and the man easily ducked away from the blow. The one on the floor was still screaming in pain, his cream jacket now a dull red. He was too busy holding his face together even to think about the gun in his pocket. But the ex-pug who'd tried the tackle remembered, and out of the corner of his eye Logan saw him move toward the writhing, blood-soaked figure. The big man moved sideways and kicked him in the head, and the man rolled away in pain. But the yellow-shirted one had dived for the rifle, and Logan saw him grab it up. Diving, he made the space behind the sofa as the rifle fired, the shot slamming through the padding of the sofa just over his head. Another shot followed, and Logan heard the high-pitched ping as it hit the back springs of the sofa. Then the hard click of a hammer hitting an empty chamber resounded. Logan came over the back of the couch like a furious bull. He dived and hit the floor as he saw the other one had gotten the .38 out of the writhing, screaming man on the floor.

"Don't move," he said, but his gun hand wavered nervously. He had them both covered and Logan was too far away to risk diving for the gun. The third one helped the bloody one to his feet. Logan glimpsed his torn, shredded face. It was nothing but raw, hanging flesh. Then the three of them were backing out of the house, through the doorway and out of sight. The one with the gun sent a parting shot at Logan, and the big man fell to one side as he saw the man's finger tighten on the trigger. The slug slammed into the wall behind him. They'd been out of sight only a split second when Julie raced across the floor to the old roll-top desk against the wall. Tearing the top drawer open, she yanked out a box of cartridges and jammed them into the rifle. She ran outside, but Logan had heard the sound of a car engine cough into life, and she was back in an instant, crying through her fury.

"They got away," she sobbed. "They got away," she sobbed. "They got away and they were the ones who killed Pops. I just know it."

"Probably," Logan agreed.

"Now you'll stay and help me, won't you?" she asked, turning eagerly. "We can find them again."

Logan shook his head, his eyes hard. "Maybe you don't go for the local cops, but they get paid for finding killers," he said. "That was a nice try back there, but the answer is still no."

He turned and started for the door.

"You're a no-good, nasty sonofabitch," she shouted after him. He nodded and kept walking.

"You're a bastard," she yelled. Logan's small smile was edged with ice.

"And a coward," she finished. He halted in the doorway once again. He knew what she meant by that last one, and he turned and looked at her. She stood glaring at him, hands on her hips, jean-clad legs spread wide apart, round breasts thrusting against the red-checked shirt. She'd called him a coward, afraid to face what she offered for his help. He let his eyes travel slowly, taking in the lines of her breasts, the softly rounded mound just above her crotch. And then, his face immobile, masking the crying ache of his body, he turned and walked out the door. She didn't know how lucky she was. With some, he'd have taken their challenge fully and then walked away. He didn't like women who tried to lay a claim on him. He and the *Urchin* did *what* they wanted, *when* they wanted and *where* they wanted. It had to be that way, until their search was over. He walked quickly, moving down to the shore and heading for town. The *Sea Urchin* rode easily on the long swells as he strode past the boat. The sight of her made him think of the letter in his cabin, the letter that had caught up to him in Wilmington. His lips tightened grimly. But first things first. Jennifer would be waiting and wondering. He quickened his pace toward town.

The car drew up to the quay in Kingdom Point Harbor and stopped before the sixty-foot, glistening-white, sleek cabin cruiser. The man in the yellow sport shirt with the red stains leaped out and waved frantically up at the deck of the boat. Two figures hurried down the gangplank, the girl in bright orange hip-huggers, bare-mid-riffed with a white halter top. She had the carefully groomed, hard brilliance of a diamond. The man had cold, blue eyes and wore a sailing blazer with gold buttons. He was tall with a face that wore a perpetual sneer. The yellow-shirted one spoke quickly and excitedly, and the man and the girl peered into the rear of the car.

"Christ, get him out of here," the girl said, turning away. "Find a hospital or get the cops—tell them he fell on a glass pitcher on the boat. Just get him away."

"I think Harry's dead," the ex-pug said. "He lost a lot of blood." The girl shuddered. "He's better off. They could never put that face together again," she said.

"Do what Doris said," the man cut in. "You say one joker with a hurricane lamp did it?" The other man nodded solemnly.

"He must be a mean bastard," the tall man commented. "He sure did a job on Harry." He turned away, taking the girl's arm and steering her back aboard the cabin cruiser. Back on the stern deck three other men appeared, dressed as deck hands in blue work shirts.

"What do we do now?" one of them asked. "Christ, Harry dead."

"We lay off the rough stuff for a while," the girl said, crisply, almost angrily. "If Harry hadn't gotten carried away with himself and killed the old man, we might be out of here already."

The girl folded her long legs into a deck chair as the others watched her. She put one beautifully manicured finger up to her finely molded lips.

"Augie said the bastard that turned Harry into sliced hamburger has a boat someplace," she said. "Maybe he was just passing by and maybe not. Maybe he's chummy with Miss Beachcomber. We'll watch the girl and find out."

The tall man nodded to the others. "That's it, then," he said. "You heard Doris. I want her watched day and night. Take turns and use glasses and stay out of sight. Just watch her and report to us."

"If she's got herself a boyfriend, she'll go to him," Doris said. "All we have to do is wait." The girl got to her feet as the others left and stretched. There was a feline grace to her body, a carefully controlled, cool grace. She looked up at the man, her eyes a gray mask.

"With Harry gone, I guess that makes you top man, Varney," she said.

"I guess so," Varney said. The girl started to brush past him when he shot an arm out and caught her by the shoulder, his fingers curling around the softness of her skin. She met his eyes with a slightly bored expression.

"And I'm not Harry, Doris," he said, his voice a controlled hiss. "I won't take what you did to Harry, shoving your ass around but never letting him get to it."

"Don't be crude, Varney," Doris said quietly.

"I'm not being crude, honey. I'm being realistic," he said. "I'm letting you know there's a new set of rules. You and me, baby, or you can cut out."

"This whole operation was my idea," Doris said.

"Sure it was. So sue me, baby. Right now I can train any good-looking chickie to do what you do. Not that I want to. You're good. You're important. But you're going to stop playing the queen."

He put a finger under her chin and lifted her face. Her smile was cold, fixed, deadly.

"What's the difference?" he asked. "We're all the same, Harry, me, you. I'm not that hard to take."

"You're vicious," Doris said.

"And Harry wasn't?" Varney laughed. "It was Harry who killed the old man."

"Harry killed because it was all he knew how to do. Killing was his way of coping with a situation. He was brutal, but you're vicious."

Varney shrugged. "And you're a sweet, little girl scout?" he said. "You're no better than the rest of us. You just like to think so. But you go on and think what you like, honey. Just make sure your gorgeous ass is ready where I want it and when I want it. That's the way it's going to be now."

Doris watched the man go down into the cabin, and she clenched her hands. He knew she wouldn't turn her back on what they had going for them. He knew she had little choice. He'd always wanted her, always watched with amused disdain as she played goddess to Harry's worship. She'd created the image for herself and had held Harry with it, kept him panting in awe of her. It'd been nice, just the way she'd wanted it, and now it was all changed. She had Varney on her back. And all because of some mean, black-hearted sonofabitch who'd ground Harry's face into oblivion. He'd pay for it, she told herself.

CHAPTER TWO

The township of Kingdom Point stretched from the harbor in a huge half-circle with the town merely the hub at the bottom center. The town itself, like the harbor, was crowded, neat, orderly, and clean. It reflected money without shouting it. The money came from the great mansions by the sea and the expensive summer homes that made up most of the township acreage. At the outer perimeter of the town, before the large estate area began, were the older frame houses. They were mostly two-family rentals now, from which the township drew most of its domestic help and labor force. Since the school districts had been consolidated, the town had expanded its library and allowed some new units to be built at the right side of the perimeter. Jennifer and the boy lived in one of these. Logan sat across from her in the neat, modestly furnished living room, his big frame making it seem smaller than it was.

They'd gone through the superficialities, the ordinary questions, and she had apologized for having to go to a staff meeting that evening. Logan told her about the old man on the beach and the girl. Jennifer watched him. She always listened and absorbed and seemed to drink things in with a kind of instant meditation that put people at ease. They were often hurt and angered by her answers. Those eyes didn't prepare them for the penetrating sharpness that was within her. The boy had come home for lunch. He'd grown taller in the six months since Logan had seen him. He had Jennifer's eyes and his father's wide smile. It was after he'd gone off to school that Jennifer brought up the old man and the girl again, leaning back on the couch, her eyes thoughtful. Logan watched the long slenderness of her legs as she crossed them, the long, smooth sweep of her thigh. She had good legs, though perhaps a shade too thin, with narrow hips and a small waist rising up to breasts that were high, softly rounded and small, but terribly appealing somehow.

"I wonder what she'll do," Jennifer said. "She's a strange, wild thing."

"She'll make out," Logan said flatly.

"The old man was her life," Jennifer said. "A woman needs someone to look after." Logan caught the faint pause, and then she hurried on to cover something she hadn't intended to phrase that way.

"There was a boy," she said. "A trucker from Hopkinsville. But he went east and that was that."

"Apparently you learn a lot of things in a library," Logan commented.

"In a town like this you do. You don't even have to ask questions. You just keep your eyes and ears open. She used to come in from time to time and talk to me. She took out books on nature and she'd bring them back with notes on the mistakes in them."

"She'll find another boyfriend and look after him," Logan commented. Jennifer's eyes told him she wasn't willing to see it so simply.

"I do agree with what she said about Chief Redmond," Jennifer said. "Anything like this would be beyond him. He'd try to sweep it under the rug. He doesn't like trouble."

Logan shrugged. "It won't be the first killing swept under a rug," he said. Jennifer turned her deep eyes on him, and he suddenly felt uncomfortable under her penetrating gaze. He let his eyes move over the small, round breasts, the narrow figure.

"You've grown harder, Logan," she commented. "Maybe you ought to stop."

"Stop what?" Logan bristled.

"Doing it all your way. Not caring. Saying to hell with everything."

"I care. You know that, Jen."

"You used to, in your own way. Now I'm not sure anymore. Maybe you're only running now, Logan." Her voice was soft, gentle, her words harsh, wounding.

"You know about running, Jen," he shot back. "When Bob died, you ran all the way here, to the Carolina Coast."

Her smile was rueful. "I guess I deserved that one," she said. "And you're right, of course. I ran, and I made a new life for myself, even with a big part of any woman's life missing."

Her soft eyes flicked over his for an instant, but he said nothing. When her husband had been alive, she and Logan had been casual friends. The world had been different then, a world with love and tenderness. He tried to shut out a laughing face with light-brown hair. Sometimes, if he were fast enough, he could do it. He didn't make it this time. With that penetrating quickness of hers, Jennifer caught the moment of pain in his eyes, and she put a hand on his, a light, soft touch.

"I didn't mean to go back and open hurts," she said. "I'm sorry. It's just that I don't like what I see in you every time we meet. Your eyes grow harder each time."

"Because I'm not sticking myself into the dirty killing of an old man. No thanks. Life's too short, and I've too many things that need finishing."

He didn't tell her of the letter aboard the *Urchin* from Sister Mary Angela in Kenya.

"Even so, you'd have stayed, once," Jennifer said.

"I'd have done a lot of things, once," Logan snapped. He looked at the slender girl in front of him. "Are you asking me to stay for this Julie?" he said, frowning.

Jennifer turned to him. "Oh, no," she said softly. "Oh, no, Logan. If ever I ask you to stay it won't be for Julie. Or for anyone else."

Logan got up. "Will I see you tomorrow?" she asked. "There's a hurricane watch on, have you heard?"

"No, I hadn't," the big man said. "If I'm here, you'll see me."

She walked to the door beside him, terribly small next to his big frame and yet terribly strong in a quiet way. At the door, they kissed without kissing, as they'd done every time he stopped by. Two people, unwilling to risk spoiling something delicate, a sweet, strange bond.

"Keep caring, Logan," she said. "That's important. And be careful of yourself."

He ran his hand down the side of her face, gently, and then he was gone, striding away, not looking back. He walked quickly through the town, past the harbor. He noted a sixty-foot glistening-white cabin cruiser. Even for Kingdom Point harbor it was a spectacular boat, all outside gloss and fancy fittings, built to impress those easily impressed. He hurried on, anxious to get aboard his own boat, away from Kingdom Point, away from the death of the old man. And away from Jennifer. He'd come closer than ever before this time, closer to moving across that line they both held so tenuously. Maybe it was because he hungered for a woman, the taste, touch, and smell of one. Maybe it was because of the girl, Julie. Her throbbing body could make a marble statue hunger. It would have been nice to hide in that thought, but the big man's uncompromising honesty wouldn't permit it. It brushed Jennifer aside and that was lying. But he wondered as he trudged along the beach. Could it ever be more than unspoken, unsurfaced with Jennifer? Once she'd been a thin connection with the past, a necessary reminder to him that once he'd believed in goodness and right and kindness, that once there had been more than the *Urchin* and himself. Maybe that was all she was now. Maybe. Sometime, perhaps, he'd find out. Only the world kept getting in the way, pushing him farther from women like Jennifer, that real world of hate and greed and senseless injustice. Maybe you only see it that way, she had once said to him. Hell, he saw it like it was. Ever since that day long ago he'd seen it like it was. The old man on the beach was dead, wasn't he? He'd been beaten to death, for all his gentleness, for all his kindness, for all his love. Shit, Logan spat out. He didn't just see it that way. It *was* that way.

He found his dinghy on the beach where he'd pulled it up far enough to escape high tide. He pushed it into the sea, the surf hardly more than a gentle ripple now. The air hung, still and heavy, and the sea was glassy calm. The sea birds swooped and circled uncertainly. It was pre-hurricane weather, all right. He tied up alongside the boat, climbed the rope ladder hanging over the starboard side, and then walked the dinghy around to the stern and made it fast on a short line. He went below decks, brought out a bottle of good Kentucky bourbon and made a Logan Special, ice, a touch of grenadine, bitters and bourbon. He sipped it and lounged in the cabin, trying to hold off the bitter, angry cloak that had wrapped itself around him as he thought about the world. The second bourbon didn't make it go away, either. What the hell, he told himself. He took the letter out of the desk drawer against the port wall. He read it again, spreading it out before him. What the hell, he repeated, a few more reminders couldn't hurt now. The memories had started to flood back while he was at Jennifer's. They would keep flooding back until he got very drunk or very angry.

Dear Logan,

I hesitated to write but you insisted with every letter that you wanted me to be honest at all times with you. Every Sister here is writing someone for help. Conditions among the people have grown terribly bad. We need medical supplies, more beds, more plasma. The new government has no funds to spare. You've been so generous in the past that this very letter seems ungrateful. It is not that, please believe me. But who can we turn to if not our old friends? I know you will do whatever you can. May God bless you.

Sister Mary Angela
Sisters of Mercy Mission

He folded the letter neatly and put it back into the desk drawer. It wouldn't be that hard to raise the money. A coat of paint and he could pick up some fishing charters. A visit to the right ports without too many questions asked could bring a job or two. And there were others, with bigger money, but he didn't want to call them. The past would be peering over his shoulder enough as it was. He poured a third Logan Special and drank it quickly, feeling the warm fire of the whiskey inside him. He turned on the radio and heard the marine forecaster's voice.

"Hurricane Phyllis could pose a serious threat," the voice crackled over the set. "The storm is now practically standing still five hundred miles off the coast of South Carolina. Winds are Force twelve at present. We cannot predict future course at this time. All ships at sea are warned to stay tuned for further advisory bulletins. Hurricane Phyllis is at present stationary, we repeat, but she is a wide storm with severe winds around the outer perimeter."

The radio went dead, and Logan turned it off. He'd heard enough for now. Phyllis was standing still and gathering ferocity. If she were still in the same general spot by morning he'd up anchor and try to crawl down the coast going south. Most likely, Phyllis would circle north when she decided to move. He started toward the galley to fry some pork chops but heard the faint sound against the starboard side, a scraping sound. Downing the remains of the bourbon, he picked up a wrench. Moving quickly, silently, he was on deck and across to the rail in seconds. He had the wrench poised in his hand when the head rose up alongside the gunwale, long, wet blond hair hanging in strings.

"It's me," she said, swinging a leg over the rail. She had on cream shorts and the bra top of a black bathing suit. He noticed the way her full breasts pushed out of the little top.

"What the hell do you want?" he growled, feeling the hard, cold anger. If she'd come out to try again to get him to stay, she'd taken the swim for nothing.

"I've got to talk to you," she said, taking deep breaths and putting a helluva strain on that little top. "I yelled from shore, but you must be deaf so I swam out."

"Talk fast. I'm busy," Logan said gruffly. Her legs were full and strong.

"You've got to go to the police station with me," she said. Logan started for her, putting one hand on the back of her neck.

"Have a nice swim back, honey," he said. "We went through this once."

"No, wait, you don't understand," she said, grabbing his hand and clinging to it. "I went there already, but Pops is gone."

Logan took his hand from her neck and frowned at her. Her eyes were serious.

"He was dead, wasn't he?" she asked solemnly.

"Of course he was dead," Logan answered. "Maybe you'd better start at the beginning. You went to the cops. What happened then?"

"I told them about Pops being killed," Julie said. "Then they went back to the beach with me, but Pops wasn't there by the dune. He wasn't anyplace. Chief Redmond and Luther are very suspicious of me. They think I'm out of my skull or I'm trying to be cute, and they want to know where Pops is. You're the only one who saw him there besides me. You've got to go and tell Chief Redmond that he was there—dead."

Logan let a long sigh escape him. "You know you're a pain in the ass," he said.

"I wish somebody else had found Pops, anybody else in the whole world but you," she blurted out angrily.

"That makes two of us, honey," he said flatly.

"Look, I don't want your lousy help," she said. "I just want you to tell those numbskulls what you saw."

Logan's lips drew tight. She didn't want his help, but he knew that one thing led to another. It always did. The three bourbons had only increased his feeling of churning meanness. The past was still kicking around in his head, and she stood there, dripping all over his deck looking like a half-drowned rabbit. "Ah, screw it all," he growled. "Let's go."

He brought the dinghy around and climbed into it after her, rowing to shore with long, powerful strokes as the girl sat silently before him, the wet shorts flattened against the small, round rise of her belly, her young, strong legs extended, almost touching his in the small boat. At the beach, he pulled the dinghy up and saw she had an old battered open-topped jeep standing there. They got in and she leaned forward to release the hand brake. He wondered if she were going to fall out of the bathing suit top. Her breasts, mounds of cream where the deep color of her tan halted, were deliciously inviting. The jeep shot forward and he grabbed the corner post to avoid being pitched out.

"Sorry," she said with satisfaction in her voice. "Why did they take Pops' body?" she asked. "Why?"

"You found that out already," Logan answered. "No body, no cops looking for suspects." It was neat and professional, he added to himself. And it made him stop and pause. Pro's wouldn't go to all this bother without a damn good reason. Maybe killing the old man had been an error on their part, but they definitely suspected something more. Everything that had happened so far pointed to the fact that this wasn't amateur night. The jeep, shuddering to a halt, interrupted his thoughts, and he saw they had stopped before a square white-washed building. Julie slipped on a sweat shirt as she hopped to the ground. Logan followed her inside the building, sparsely furnished, with a large wooden desk in one corner of the receiving room. He saw another room leading off to the right and a corridor to the left. The man got up from behind the desk, a big raw-boned man with a heavy jaw and black hair. His small eyes glittered when he saw Julie.

"I'm back, Luther," the girl said. "Tell the chief, please."

Luther's eyes devoured the girl in one quick glance. Then Luther turned his small, mean, pig's eyes on him. His gray police-man's shirt and silver badge tried its best to make him look natty. It failed. The man rose and walked toward Logan, his arms long and loose.

"What's your name?" he said slowly. Logan forced himself to keep calm. He didn't want any part of this, and he didn't want to make it worse than it was. But Luther's type set the meanness inside him churning faster. The man exuded that special kind of arrogance found in minor authorities with minor minds.

"Logan," the dark-eyed man said, his lips hardly moving, his eyes warning Luther. But Luther had enough trouble reading words. Reading people was far beyond him.

"Well, now, Logan," he drawled. "What are you doing in Kingdom Point?"

"Leaving. As fast as I can," Logan said. "Not that it's any of your damn business."

"Don't get smart with me, mister," Luther growled, squinting his little eyes.

"Don't ask me any dumb questions," Logan said. "I came here because the girl asked me to back up her story. I saw the old man, and he was dead. That's it, pal. You take it from there."

Logan started to turn, but the man raised his voice. "Not so fast there," Luther said. "Chief! Can you come out here?"

Logan felt the angry irritation rising inside him, and he shot Julie a glance. She was watching him. A man emerged from the adjoining room, older than Luther, beefy-faced and red-necked with a paunch covering a powerful body.

"This is the feller Julie told us about," Luther said. "I asked him a question, and he gave me a smart-ass answer."

The police chief's eyebrows lifted a fraction, and he sauntered toward Logan. Logan saw the man had experience, if nothing else, the kind of experience which allowed him to read men on a primitive level at least.

"We don't like smart answers here," he said, his voice quiet. Logan's irritation was rising close to the exploding point.

"I'm all choked up about that," he said, The beefy-faced man had cold, blue eyes and they held Logan's hard glance.

"Luther asked you what you were doing here in Kingdom Point. Julie said you had a boat and you dropped anchor offshore last night. Now you can answer us or you can get yourself a jail cell."

"For what reason?" Logan asked, his eyes unmoving.

"I'll think of somethin'," the police chief said. Logan smiled— a tight, hard smile. He almost laughed. It was going just the way he thought it would go. Trouble. One thing leading to another. He wasn't about to drop Jennifer's name into this and his own stubbornness had taken over. That and his inner anger.

"I'm waiting," Chief Redmond said.

"Don't make it a total loss," Logan answered. "Go screw yourself while you're at it."

"Damn it, Logan, why can't you just answer?" Julie cut in. "He's visiting someone here in Kingdom Point, chief. Now can we get back to what happened to Pops?"

The telephone rang in the other room and the police chief tore his hard, blue eyes from Logan. I'm waiting for that call," he said. "But I'll be back. I'm not finished with you."

As the man disappeared, Luther moved to stand in front of Logan. "Now, suppose you tell us just who you're visiting here in Kingdom Point," he said, his little eyes glittering.

"Suppose you go to hell," Logan said coldly.

"He's visiting Jennifer Holden," Julie said. "Who cares?"

Logan grimaced, and shot her an angry look. The little bitch knew he didn't want it tossed around, but she was only interested in placating the cops. Logan felt his anger start to churn as a slow smile oozed across Luther's face.

"Well, what do you know," he said. "Jennifer Holden." A nasty oil coated every syllable. "Cur little librarian entertaining visiting sailormen," Luther went on. "It's sure a surprising world."

Logan hit him. He caught Luther on the point of the jaw and felt the bone splinter. Luther flew across the room, hit the old desk, catapulted across it, and crashed to the floor on the other side, striking the desk chair. He made a hell of a loud crash as he hit, and Chief Redmond charged into the room seconds later.

"What the hell's going on here?" he barked, one hand on his gun. He looked at the inert form of his patrolman on the floor, the desk chair across the man's back.

"He slipped on something and fell across the desk," Logan said mildly. Chief Redmond took a cup from a paper dispenser, filled it at a water cooler, and threw the water into Luther's face. He did it twice again before Luther blinked his eyes. The chief helped him to his feet.

"Sonofabitch hit me," Luther gasped, putting his head down on the desk.

"Nothing of the sort," Logan smiled pleasantly. "He must have a concussion. I told you he slipped and fell." The big man turned his deep, probing eyes on Julie. "Did you see him slip and fall?" he asked. Juli paused a second and then answered.

"That's what I saw," she said.

"Sonofabitch hit me," Luther repeated, resting one hand against his swelling jaw. "I'm goin' over to Doc Green."

"Two against one," Logan smiled at the police chief. "You'd have trouble making a case."

"You get out of here, the police chief growled. "You go with him, Julie. And don't come back."

"My pleasure," Logan said, his smile thin. He walked outside, conscious of the girl's seething anger as she strode alongside him. When they reached the jeep she exploded into fury.

"Damn you!" she said, eyes ablaze. "What'd you have to go and get everybody mad for? Why couldn't you just answer Luther's questions?"

"I didn't come to answer questions," Logan said.

"Why'd you have to hit him just because he mentioned Jennifer Holden entertaining you?"

"I didn't like the way he said it."

"You're just naturally mean, aren't you?"

"No. I work at it. It's more fun that way."

The night was wrapping itself around the town. Logan followed Julie into the jeep. She swung the car back toward the beach, the headlights stabbing into the darkness. It was black when they reached the dinghy. Logan swung out of the jeep and started to pull the boat toward the water.

"Good luck, Julie," he said.

"What do you mean good luck?" the girl shot back. "You're not just going off, are you?"

"Keep watching, honey," he said, pushing the dinghy into the water.

"After what you did?" she asked. "After fixing it so they won't do anything?"

"Work on Luther," Logan called back. "He'll do whatever you say, doll. Soon as he gets his jaw fixed."

Logan looked back at her, standing at the water's edge. He could feel the throbbing, pulsating rage in her, a rage he could turn into wild passion, he knew. But he kept rowing, just as he'd turned away at the doorway. He had things to do. He'd find another woman easily enough, one without conditions or claims. He was halfway to the *Sea Urchin* when he heard her voice come across the water.

"Bastard," she yelled. He grinned in the dark.

"That's me," he called back and heard the sound of the jeep's engine coughing into life. He reached the *Urchin,* tied the dinghy up at the stern and switched on the radio as he went into the galley. The pork chops were waiting, and he had them frying and crackling in a few minutes. Phyllis, the marine forecaster said, was still more or less in one spot, gathering intensity.

"An extremely dangerous storm," the forecaster said. "Air currents indicate the hurricane will move toward the coast when its forward motion is resumed. The hurricane watch remains in force and all ships are advised to stay tuned for further bulletins."

Logan poured himself a bourbon on the rocks and went on deck. Unless things changed overnight, he'd still weigh anchor in the morning and head down toward the gulf ports.

Logan stretched, finished his drink and went to bed in the aft cabin. Sleep would keep his mind from the throbbing, raw beauty of Julie and the soft magnetism of Jennifer. Maybe he shouldn't have stopped at Kingdom Point this time, he mused idly. Nothing had really gone right this time. His visit with Jennifer had been too full of the things that penetrate and hurt. And memories he kept hidden away.

And the old man on the beach was dead. Logan let sleep wash over him, dulling, numbing sleep that turned off the world for a little while.

The big man slept, naked except for shorts, and the open porthole let the warm, still air into the cabin. But Logan slept like a jungle cat sleeps, with an extra sense constantly tuned to danger, a sudden sound, a footstep, a movement in the air. He didn't know how long he'd been asleep when his eyes snapped open and felt the cold tingling of his skin. He lay still, and then he heard it, the faint scraping sound on the deck above. Swinging from the bed on silent, bare feet, he moved with instant grace, taking the few steps of the companionway in one effortless bound. He halted, crouched, as he saw her moving across the deck on tiptoe toward the forward cabin, leaving little pools of water behind her. He moved forward and kicked out, catching her round little rear with his foot. She yelled as she went sprawling across the deck, and he saw the small oilskin bag roll off to one side.

"Goddamn it, what are you doing here again?" the big man yelled. The girl looked up at him from where she lay on the deck, her blond hair wet, hanging behind her and held by a hair clip, the blouse pressed tight against her skin, outlining the curved peaks of her breasts, the tiny pointed tips.

"I couldn't stay at the house," she said, pushing herself to her feet. "I tried to but I couldn't. Not alone, not with everything reminding me of Pops. And every little noise made me jump. I was afraid those goons might come back. I just had to get away— for a while, anyway. You can take me and drop me off someplace, any place."

"Forget it," Logan said. She moved toward him, her wet clothes clinging to her every curve.

"You owe me that much, damn it," she said.

"I owe you?" Logan frowned. "For what? I went with you to back up your story about the old man."

"And if I hadn't backed *you* up, you'd be in jail now for hitting Luther," she said.

"So we're even. So butt out."

"No. I'm not going back there."

Logan saw her eyes moving over his chest, down the hard-packed muscles of his body, and her eyes smoldered with something that went beyond stubborn defiance. "Please, let me stay," she said. "I won't be any trouble."

"You'll be nothing but trouble," Logan muttered and his hands tightened with the desire to reach out and touch her full, rounded breasts. She was less than an arm's length away, her eyes holding his in the dark of the moonless night. She was a stray cat and a simmering strumpet, a waif and a wanton hellion, all at once. He put a hand out and curled it around the back of her neck. It was thin and soft. He pulled her to him. There was a delicious, wet-hot smell to her. She offered no resistance. Her full lips, parted, beckoned invitingly and he leaned down to them, pressing them open wider with his. His tongue sent its own instant message as it circled her mouth, quickly, with darting movements, and he felt her go rigid. He put one hand on her breast, the wetness of her blouse a thin layer of insulation between his fingers and the warmth of her softness. She shivered, but she didn't pull away, and he felt her shoulder muscles grow tight. Yet she didn't move away, and he pulled back. Her eyes were open, wide, watching him.

"Still want to stay?" he said.

"I'm staying," she answered, her voice hardly more than a whisper.

"I'll throw you off at the first real port we reach."

"I know."

He opened the buttons of the wet blouse and let his hand rest against the warmth of her breast. He heard the sharp, inward sound of her breath.

"I'm not getting involved."

"I heard you."

He moved his hand down on her breast, feeling the deep fullness of her. His mouth was against her cheek.

"You can still go."

"I'm staying. I'm not going back. Not for a while."

Her words were like a final seal on an agreement and he felt his better judgment explode in the whirlpool of his desires. His hand ripped at the brassiere, pulling it down. Her arms encircled him, and she pressed her body against his, pulling his head down her. The big man picked up the girl in his arms, and carried her into the aft cabin.

He flung her on the bed like a sack of wheat and as she rolled, she rolled free of her blouse and came at him with a furious passion, clawing at his shorts, pulling them from him. Her hands were thirsting, grasping, and he came to her with his head buried into her breasts, pressing their soft, warm tips to his lips, pulling gently on them and feeling their pink points rising. She kicked her shorts free, and he felt her young, strong legs clasp themselves around him, the soft warmth of her belly pressing up to him. Logan was caught up in the sweet pain of his exploding needs, but the girl seemed to be aflame with a release of tensions. She wanted little gentleness, little subtlety, and she grabbed and clawed and pressed herself up to the big man's muscular body, twisting her hips so that she could take him in at once. As he moved to her, she clutched at him and, arms tight around his neck, cried out in pure joyous pleasure.

"Oh, yes, yes, Christ, yes!" she gasped as he matched her own frenzy and held her there, just a heartbeat from the peak of peaks, letting her down and bringing her up again until she was crying out in an endless chain of gasps and finally her cries were cries of pleading. "Oh, take me over, damn it, oh, Christ, take me over," Julie screamed in his ear, her body all frenzied passion, reaching for the top, trying desperately to hurry that which only he could hurry and then, with a final explosion of ecstasy, he thrust fully and deeply into her, holding himself against the very inner depths of her, and her cry was a song of towering fulfillment. Beneath his legs, strong and pressing down, her body leaped and flung itself upwards, arching again and again in a seemingly uncontrollable frenzy. Finally, she subsided in a series of quivering motions. He tried to move from her but her legs tightened again, and she moaned, eyes closed. "Oh, no, no, stay with me, oh, God, stay with me," she said. He moved slowly now, like the slow roll of the surf against the sand on a calm day, and she moaned and gasped and shook with small ripples of pleasure. Finally, he felt her legs fall aside, and he turned and lay beside her. He felt her hand stealing down to hold him, and with eyes closed, she turned her face to his ear.

"You're something different, Logan," she breathed. "Christ, you're something different." She fell aside and lay on her back, her full, round breasts moving steadily up and down. Logan raised himself on one elbow to look at her. She was asleep, he saw, her hand limply holding him, spent, exhausted.

He lay back in the contentment of a need fulfilled and a promise of more to come. He would do just what he said, throw her off at the first port they put in. But before that moment, he would drink of her wild, sensuous body again. It had been a day of brutal death, violence, anger, and hurt. Perhaps it was no more fitting that it should come to a close in an explosion of hunger, a meeting that was more frenzy than loving, sex as violent and turbulent as the day had been.

CHAPTER THREE

The new day came in on a blanket of still, thick air with the sun a blurred, diffused red. Logan stirred as the light crept tentatively through the porthole. He turned and looked at the girl beside him. Even asleep, her body had a throbbing lushness to it, and he let his eyes rove over the rounded rise of her belly, the round undersides of her breasts, so full and womanly with such small, pink little-girl tips. She stirred, raised one leg and half-turned in her sleep. Her fleshy opulence seemed to send out its own currents, and he felt himself wanting to move his body against her. He swung silently from the bed. There'd be time for that later. Naked, he went across the cabin and turned on the ship's radio.

On the bed, Julie opened her eyes just enough to see through them and watched the tall man's naked form as he stood at the porthole window and peered out, went to the doorway and glanced up through the opening of the companionway. She let her eyes roam across his figure, the powerful pectoral muscles, the easy grace of him, the maddeningly stirring maleness of him. She felt him against her as he'd been last night, felt him moving inside her, felt his lips pulling on her breasts and her body began to stir and ache at once. She was no worldly sophisticate, no creature of infinite experience, but she didn't have to be to know that she'd never be made love to again like this man had made love to her. He was a strange one, this Logan. Hard, immovable, living in his own world. But, she mused, her mind stirring to sudden life, perhaps she could be part of that world.

She could understand a man like him. The years of lonely living with Pops and the sea and the sand had given her the gift to understand the lone things of the world and this big man was one of them. She smiled. Maybe she'd even have a surprise or two for him. The sound of the marine forecaster on the radio interrupted her thoughts, and she listened to the words crackling into the air.

"Hurricane Phyllis is moving toward the Carolina coast at a very slow rate but is expected to pick up speed. Phyllis has become an exceedingly dangerous storm with Force ten winds around the outer perimeter and one hundred and fifty mile winds at the center. All shipping is advised to stay in port or to head for shelter until the course of the hurricane can be more exactly charted."

"Damn," Logan muttered, shutting off the radio. If Phyllis hit directly, Kingdom Point hadn't the kind of protection needed. Bayville would be better, but it was always so damned crowded there that getting in was uncertain. He knew just the place, a little cove with high protective walls and a narrow entrance. But it was a day's trip north and he wanted to go south. He'd wait a little longer. If Phyllis changed direction he might still be able to stick to his original plan of crawling southward along the coast. He walked back to the bed and saw Julie watching him. He put on his shorts and trousers as he took in her loveliness. She stretched, moving her lush body with soft grace, inviting him. He grinned. All in time, honey, he said to himself. Right now he wanted to check over the *Urchin* and see that everything was tight and in place. Even if Phyllis didn't hit them directly, they'd be sideswiped and that would be bad enough.

"You'll find breakfast in the galley," he said. "I like my eggs sunny-side up. Bacon and coffee."

When he walked from the cabin, she swung her legs over the side of the bed. He went out into the morning sun and the still air. As he started to put away loose equipment, leaving out two deck chairs, stowing away ropes and snap-shut canvas covers, he smelled the bracing aroma of coffee and bacon. Soon Julie appeared with the breakfast tray. He quickly noted that her breasts moved freely under the blouse, unconfined, swaying and pressing their little tips against the thin fabric. She wore the shorts again, tight and provocative on her firm little seat.

They sat down to eat.

"Do you like anyone or anything?" Julie asked. Logan's smile was hard, his dark eyes moving across the water.

"Lots of things," he said. "People are at the bottom of the list, though."

"You didn't seem to have much trouble last night," she snapped.

"That's another game, sweetie, and you know it." His eyes probed into her, a small frown on his brow.

"You got another name beside Julie?" he asked.

"Banntry," she said.

"Julie Banntry," he said, turning the name over in his mind. "How'd you hook up with the old man, Julie Banntry?"

"My mother was sick, back in Towerville, across the state," Julie said. "She sent me to him for the summer. I was twelve. She died while I was here, and I stayed on."

"Nobody else to take you in?"

"Nobody that wanted me," she said, suddenly all waif again. "My relatives all had too many kids. They didn't need another twelve-year-old around. We're alike, Logan, you know that? We've learned to be loners, to go our own way."

Logan grunted and his eyes narrowed. He could see where she was heading. Like all women, she calculated constantly. Only it wasn't really calculation with them. It was part of them, built into them.

"And that's the way it's going to stay, honey," he growled and saw the small flicker of annoyance in her eyes. "You won't have any trouble finding someone to want you now."

"Who are you, Logan?" she asked. "I've seen a lot of sea bums, but you're not one of them. And this boat, it's a lot different when you're on it. Who're you hiding from?"

"Not a who, a what. I hide from being bothered."

"Like having to help someone."

"That's right," he said, standing up. "Wash the dishes and put them away. Then come on deck, and I'll give you something else to do." He watched her go below and knew that her submissive obedience was a strain on her. He'd seen her flaring temper, sampled her chameleonlike swift changes of mood already. She was utterly female, from the smoldering lush beauty of her to the pathetic appeal she could exude. And female in her inability to read signs, to think that anyone could be beyond her reach. He smiled inwardly. What the hell, it'd be fun for a few days, anyhow.

A sleek, glistening-white motor cruiser moved out of Kingdom Point harbor. A girl stood on the forward deck, in tailored white slacks and a black jersey top, every blond hair in place, sparkling with her own light. She was listening to the tall man in the brass-buttoned navy-blue jacket. She seemed to be ignoring him.

"Damn it, Doris," he said. "The boys watched her swim out to her boyfriend's boat last night. What have you got against moving in?"

The girl turned and fastened the man with a cool, steady gaze. "You growing deaf, Varney?" she said. "I told you last night, we should wait till they make their move and then act. We've been too quick with the rough stuff right along."

"Waiting bothers me, Doris," Varney said. "You know that." He turned to her. "Waiting for anything bothers me." He smiled, a thin, knife-edged smile. The girl ignored the remark.

"I'd think you'd be happy to let me get at her boyfriend," Varney went on, the edge still in his voice. "After all, if it hadn't been for him you'd still have Harry here in my place."

Doris gave Varney a smile that dripped with venom. "That's why I don't want to see anything go wrong," she said.

"Nothing will go wrong, baby," Varney said, his eyes hard. The gleaming-white motor cruiser, clear of the small harbor, gathered speed and sent showers of spray cascading into the air as she turned left and moved along the beachfront. Varney, lifting binoculars to his eyes, saw the paint-chipped hull of the *Sea Urchin* looming just ahead.

"They've weighed anchor!" he exclaimed excitedly. "They're trying to get away."

"They don't seem in much of a hurry," Doris commented acidly as she watched the other boat drifting lazily in the gentle swells.

"Tony," the man called to the helmsman. "Swing on her port side. Keep her between you and the beach."

Aboard the *Sea Urchin*, Logan watched the glistening-white cruiser coming up at full speed, and his eyes narrowed as the hair on the back of his neck rose—his own personal alarm bell that had never been wrong. He'd weighed anchor to put a few hundred yards more water between himself and the beach. He'd planned to drop anchor again, but now he didn't. He saw the other craft start to swing out to come alongside him on the port side. Sweeping his glance along the rail he saw the five men lining up, saw the carbines in the hands of two of them. A little farther on, he picked out the shapely figure in white slacks and black jersey top. A blue-jacketed man stood beside her.

"Something wrong?" Julie said, coming on deck and looking up at Logan's narrowed, hard eyes watching the approaching boat.

"Yes, I think so," he said. "Anyone see you swim aboard last night?"

"Not that I know of," she answered.

"No, not that you know of," he said. "I never should've let you stay."

"Make sense," she snapped, anger flaring in her voice.

"Maybe they'll make sense for you," he shot back, nodding to the approaching cruiser. "They're not out for a sail. They're coming for us. I can tell by the way she's moving."

Slow realization started to move into her round blue eyes. "You mean the goons who killed Pops?" she gasped. "The ones who came to the house yesterday?"

He shrugged. "I've got no friends with fancy motor cruisers around here. Maybe you have."

She looked out at the oncoming boat, fear in her eyes. With startling abruptness, Logan turned and moved into the pilot house, taking the few steps to it in one bound. She followed and saw him flip a switch on the instrument panel. The dull throb of the boat's engines flooded the air, deep, powerful.

"The engines are idling now," he said. "Get over here and stay by this wheel. If I tell you to hit the switch, you flip it over to full, understand?" She nodded. "And hold the wheel just where she is, with the top of it lined up with that little arrow on the compass."

Logan glanced out to see the white cruiser slow to a halt as she swung around to come alongside him. "Just do what I told you to do when I say so," he said. He stepped out of the pilot house and went to the rail. Inside his cabin he had a big Colt Python .357 Magnum. He decided to leave it there for the moment. The gleaming cruiser had come to a dead halt alongside them with perhaps ten feet or so between them. Logan moved to the *Urchin's* rail. The tall man with the blue jacket called out, and Logan let his eyes travel over the man's cold face, then move to the girl. He took in her curving breasts, the nice long line of her thighs beneath the tight white slacks and the cool interest in her eyes. How large a role did she play in this, he wondered. Sweeping the men again, he saw the two ex-pugs that had been at the house. Cream jacket was missing, he noted with grim pleasure.

"We don't want any more trouble," the tall man called. "Just hand it over, and you can go your way."

"I'm going my way, cousin," Logan said. "And I don't know what the hell you want."

"Either you or blondie in there knows," the man said. "Are you going to play ball or do we come aboard?"

Logan's eyes scanned the five men at the rail. One of the two with carbines stood at the near end of the line.

"You want to come aboard?" he said. "I'll give you a line."

He picked up one end of a mooring line and tossed it with a quick motion at the man with the carbine. The man, reacting automatically, almost dropped the rifle as he reached out to grab the rope that flew at him.

"Hold onto it," Logan called and the man, tucking the rifle under his arm, curled the rope around his wrist. Logan hissed through clenched teeth, not turning toward the pilot house.

"Hit that switch," he said and paused a second to see Julie throw the switch out of the corner of his eye and then grab the wheel with both hands. He yanked the rope hard and suddenly and saw the man pitch forward, hit the rail and go over in a head-long plunge from the cruiser. He hit the water as the full force of the *Urchin's* wake swept over him, engulfing him in a cascade of swirling water, pulling him under and turning him over and over. It had all taken not much more than a second and Logan flattened himself on the deck as the initial surprise aboard the cruiser gave way to a burst of rifle fire. But the *Sea Urchin's* powerful engines had taken hold to send the boat leaping forward, and the shots flew harmlessly overhead. Logan got to his feet and ran to the pilot house where Julie sat at the wheel, fingers clenched around it, eyes wide with determination mixed with fear. He took the wheel from her and looked back to see the cruiser had gathered speed and was giving chase. He slowed somewhat and adjusted the synchrometer readings to assure himself maximum power. He let the cruiser come up on him and then shot the

Urchin forward in a burst of raw power that threw her wake up onto the white vessel's foredeck. Julie, pressed against the far wall of the pilot house, saw Logan's small grin.

"Jesus, what have you got in this thing, airplane engines?" she asked. Logan chuckled.

"Just a little extra power," he answered. He knew that aboard the white motor cruiser the same question was being asked. Logan cut back again on the power and once more the other vessel moved closer but this time, as she closed in, he spun the wheel and the *Urchin* turned in a tight circle. He saw the white craft try to follow suit and only succeed in swinging wide in a clumsy arc. He kept the *Urchin* in the tight circle and watched the figures aboard the other vessel rush to the starboard side. Then he heard the sharp, staccato sound of a submachine gun and he felt the thud of the bullets as they slammed into the bottom section of the pilot house, just below the line of the windows, sending up slivers of wood.

"Goddamn it!" Logan cursed. He spun the wheel and pulled the *Urchin* out of her tight circle, sending her straight at the cruiser's white side. He saw the man at the wheel, unnerved and outmaneuvered already, come apart and frantically spin his wheel to port. The long, sleek vessel heeled precariously as she swung about, sending those on the deck stumbling and sliding along the rail. Logan let the *Urchin* drive past the stern of the cruiser while it yawed and floundered, lost headway and direction. By the time she swung back Logan had put plenty of water between them. But the machine gun had added a new element to the game. He could outmaneuver them easily, and keep a lead on the straightaway. But he couldn't do battle, not just himself and Julie against a submachine gun and God knows what else. He peered back to see that the white vessel had gathered herself and had taken up the pursuit. Julie poked her head out of the pilot house window and saw the sleek white vessel roaring after them.

"What do you want to do?" she asked.

"Throw you overboard," he snapped.

"So they saw me come aboard last night," the girl answered angrily. "That doesn't mean anything."

"It does to them," Logan said. "And are you sure it doesn't to you?" Julie's lips tightened. She hesitated a brief moment before answering. He wondered if it was just anger or something more.

"It meant I wanted to get away," she said. "Maybe you'd like me to save you the trouble and just jump overboard?" Her sarcasm was defensive.

"Use either side, honey," Logan snapped. He saw the blaze of anger in her blue eyes.

"You never stop being a bastard do you, Logan?"

"I did last night," he growled. "And now look." He peered back at the pursuing boat to see she had gained a little, not enough to worry about.

"Can you outrun them?" Julie asked.

"Not enough to lose them," he said. "I'm going to put in at Bayville."

"Bayville?" she exploded incredulously. "They'll come right in after us."

"I know," he said. "But in a harbor jammed full of boats all they'll be able to do is sit there and watch us. As soon as that damned hurricane decides which way it's going, I'll decide what we do next. Now shut up and let me move this boat."

Julie lapsed into silence, and went out onto the deck. Logan checked the pursuing vessel, gunning the *Urchin* just enough to keep the distance the same between them. They'd be in Bayville in an hour or two. Damn, he swore to himself. He should have sent her away last night. But he hadn't, and now his pursuers were convinced he either had or knew about whatever it was they were after. He looked down at Julie on the deck, the wind pressing her blouse tight against the soft contours of her full breasts. She glanced up at him, and he saw the glint of smug satisfaction in her eyes. Damn her, he swore under his breath. In the same way she got to you with her swift changes of mood, she pulled you into her problems, and she'd managed to pull him in deeper, perhaps too deeply to turn aside now. And she was pleased with herself for it. He felt the cold anger building inside him, a cold anger at her, at the bastards chasing him in the white boat, at the world in general. He didn't want any part of this. He had things to do, things important to him. And this wasn't one of them. So if he was in too deep, he'd cut his way out as quickly and as ruthlessly as he could.

He looked back at the other craft, and he thought about the girl he'd seen on her. Where did she fit in, he wondered. She had a cool, disdainful air to her, even in the few seconds he'd watched her. He eased off on the throttle as Bayville harbor came into sight. Casting a glance behind, he saw that the motor cruiser continued racing toward them at full speed. His faint smile was cold, and he steered for the harbor mouth. The other craft had closed the distance by the time he reached the harbor, but now they were already in full view of the quays and piers jutting out from the curved shoreline. There'd be no room to find docking space, but that didn't matter. He moved slowly into the harbor, keeping one eye on the sleek cruiser as she nosed in after him. He saw a spot at the outside edge of the boats moored offshore, in a direct line from the harbor mouth. He swung the *Sea Urchin* around and dropped anchor. The long, white cruiser reversed engines, moved to the right and found a spot almost directly opposite them but on the other side of the harbor channel. Logan went into the aft cabin and took out the big Colt Python .357 Magnum, stuck it into his belt, got a pair of field glasses, and went up on deck. He trained them on the cruiser and made a fast count of those aboard. He came up with seven, besides the girl and the cold-faced man in the navy-blue blazer. Allowing for one or two more possibly below decks that made at least ten. But there had been two more, he smiled grimly. He put down the glasses and saw Julie watching him.

"Now what?" she said. "We just wait around?"

"We just wait around," he said. He went below and turned on the weather forecast. Phyllis was still moving very slowly directly toward the coast, and Logan's lips tightened grimly. There was still time for decisions, at least twenty-four hours. He opened a bottle of bourbon and took out two glasses.

"Relax, Julie," he said, handing her a glass. "We might as well enjoy ourselves." He saw her eyes darken, and he knew she got the message. It was mid-afternoon and the pre-hurricane stillness in the air continued. The harbor, without the winds of the open sea, was hot and Logan took off his shirt as he relaxed on the deck, aware that they were no doubt watching from the cruiser. He lifted a glass high, gestured toward the other vessel, and downed the drink.

Aboard the white boat, Varney cursed and put down his binoculars. "The bastard," he swore. Doris's lips formed a slow smile. "He's a cool one, all right," she said. "And that little old boat is something more than it looks. But you found that out, didn't you, Varney?"

The man turned to her and his eyes glittered. "Don't give me any of that superior shit you used to hand Harry," he growled. "You've got as much to lose as any of us. If that damned hurricane hits before we get the stuff and get out of here, God knows what'll happen."

Doris's eyes held their cool, infuriating disdain that she knew stabbed deeply. "You wanted to play it your way, remember, darling?" she said. "I said to hang back until they made their move. But you had to go chasing out after them."

"How do we know she didn't bring the stuff to the boat when she swam out last night?" Varney asked angrily. Doris shrugged. "Maybe she did. But we could have followed them till we got the right spot to move in. Now he's got us boxed in here where we can't make a move. Not your kind of move, anyway."

"What do you mean by that?" Varney asked quickly. Doris leaned on the rail, and her eyes narrowed as she looked across the harbor channel at the *Sea Urchin*. A faint smile touched her patrician features.

"He's cute, mean, and dangerously competent," she said. She turned to the cold-faced man. "Which all means he's a smart cookie. And, if he's as smart as I think he is, he can be made to listen to reason. I think I could get him to cooperate."

The tall man's eyes grew small as he turned her words over in his mind. He smiled slowly. "You going to try waving it in front of him like you did with Harry?" he said. "Suppose he wants you to come across first?"

"That's my problem, Varney," Doris said, not bothering to conceal the hatred in her eyes. "You want the stuff. I think I can get it for us. That's all."

"That's right, baby," Varney said. "I don't think you can do it, but it's worth a try. I'll have Augie row you over."

Varney turned and walked forward along the deck. Doris looked out across the water again. The girl might pose a problem, she mused. But then perhaps she wouldn't. She remembered the big man's eyes as they flicked over her. She waited, watching the dinghy being lowered into the water, and then went down the single-curved ladder at the side of the boat.

Logan saw the rowboat moving toward the *Urchin* as the afternoon turned to dusk. He didn't move. "We're going to have company," he said to the girl. She got up at once and looked over the rail. Logan went to his cabin, opened a drawer and took out a double-edged knife with a weighted handle. He put it into his belt next to the big Colt Python. When he went back on deck the rowboat was alongside, and he heard the girl call out. He looked down at her and saw the beauty that lay behind the cool, contained facade she wore.

"I want to come aboard," she called up to him. "I think we ought to talk."

Logan lowered a rope ladder, and she reached out and started to climb up. He stopped her halfway up. The man had begun to climb up after her, holding the boat's line in his hand.

"Just you, honey," Logan growled. She halted, looked down at the man and spoke to him.

"It's all right, Augie," she said. "Just wait for me."

She climbed up the rest of the way, and Logan let her clamber over the rail by herself.

"Thanks for the help," she glared at him. He looked down at the man in the rowboat. "Move over to the port side," he said and watched as the man rowed around the *Urchin*. On the port side he was away from the eyes of the harbor and of the white cruiser. Logan took the knife from his belt, raised it and threw it with speed, strength, and accuracy. It hurtled silently through the air and hit the man in the rowboat at the top of his breastbone, going in at an angle to pierce his neck. He uttered a short, strangled cry, half rose, hands clutched to his neck, and then toppled forward and over the side of the rowboat. Logan looked at the girl and saw her eyes darken with surprise and shock.

"What was that for?" she asked, brows knitted in a deep frown.

"Cutting down the odds," Logan smiled pleasantly. Her eyes held his for a long moment, and then she shook her head. There was almost a tint of admiration in her voice as she spoke.

"You are a mean, no-good hard-nose, aren't you?" she said. "You're the one that sliced up Harry with the hurricane lamp, aren't you?"

"Harry killed the old man on the beach, didn't he?" Logan countered. Doris smiled.

"I guess neither of us likes to answer questions, do we?" she said. Logan shrugged. "Depends on the questions."

"May we go below?" the girl asked. "I'm Doris. And you?"

"Logan," the big man said, starting down into the cabin. He saw Julie move to follow and heard Doris speak, cool contempt in her voice.

"Not you, dearie," she said. "This is private."

Logan smiled inwardly. He didn't know what her game was, but he wanted to ler her try it out, anyway. "Stay on deck," he said to Julie and saw her about to explode. Only the cold, icy command in his eyes held her, and she subsided into a silent, seething rage. Logan went below and pulled the cabin door shut after Doris. She glanced around the cabin with cool, appreciative eyes.

"This funny little boat is quite something, isn't she?" she said, taking in the rosewood paneling and the Burma teak cabin floor. She turned her eyes on Logan.

"And I think maybe you're quite something," she said.

"Thanks," he said flatly. "But you didn't come here to admire my boat. Get on with it, honey."

Doris sat down on the edge of the bed and studied the big man's hard, lined face, handsome with a driving, dangerous recklessness to it. He radiated an electricity that was more than pure animal magnetism, and she was glad she'd come. She didn't see this man with the lush little creature on deck. Not for more than a few nights.

"I came because I thought perhaps you were a reasonable man," she said. "I thought perhaps you'd be interested in an offer."

"Maybe," he said. "But first you tell me what this is all about."

"Stop playing games, Logan," the girl said tartly. "You know what it's all about."

"You make believe I don't and tell me," he said. "Start from the beginning. I don't like coming in at the middle of anything."

Doris's lips pursed, and her eyes held Logan's coldly.

"The old man found something very important to us," she said. "It fell from a small private plane flying low across the beach. The old man was seen picking it up. He took it and hid it someplace. We didn't know who he was or where he lived, but we figured he might come back to the beach. Harry waited for him and got carried away questioning him."

A small smile flickered across Logan's face. The girl's story had fitted into what he suspected already. Her breasts, pointed peaks pushing toward him, held his attention for a moment. Her cool, contained disdain was infuriatingly tantalizing. With her every movement and glance she seemed to dare one to pierce her outer shell. The very perfection of her features added to the superior attitude that cloaked her.

"What's your offer?" he asked blandly.

"A thousand dollars," she said. "You give us what you have of ours, get your thousand and everybody's happy."

Logan smiled. "I don't need a thousand dollars," he said. "Try something else. Or raise the ante."

Doris leaned back on her elbows on the bed and saw the big man's eyes drink in her figure. His powerful shoulders rippled as he moved toward her and she felt the overwhelming strength of him, the maleness of him. She started to get up but a big hand pushed her back down. The hand stayed on her chest, holding her on the bed.

"I'm not for sale," she said.

"I didn't say you were," he answered. "Don't you ever do any-thing because you feel like it?"

"I only feel like it on special occasions with special people."

"All flash and no fire, eh?"

"I didn't say that," she answered, and saw his big form bend-ing over her, saw his face coming down to blot out her vision and then his lips were on hers, forcing her mouth open roughly and she felt his tongue caressing her. Doris felt her hands move invol-untarily and a surging desire coursed through her body.

"This is a special occasion of a sort," Logan said to her, mov-ing his lips from hers. She scooted up on the bed, putting more distance between them. The moment of feeling had passed from her eyes. They were cold and contained again, and Logan permitted himself a small smile.

"Okay, you're not for sale, but I am," he said. Her contained disdain had aroused an angry desire in him. But it was more than that. She was one of those responsible for the old man's death. And it was nothing to her, a passing incident. Death was nothing, brutality no more. She took pride in being able to avoid giving out. To make her come across would be to defeat her, to strike back for the old man in the only way that would reach this beautiful, unprincipled little bitch. He had wanted no part of this whole damned thing, but he was in it and he'd hit back at every one of them where it would hurt the most.

"You want to buy what I can tell you?" he asked, pulling her toward him savagely. "You know the price."

Doris's eyes held his for a long moment and then suddenly she was smiling. Maybe this could work out in more ways than one, she told herself. This big bastard could take care of Varney for her. He might even fit in with a new set-up. She'd give him something to come back for.

"What about your girlfriend on deck?" she asked, starting to pull off the black jersey. Logan got up and went out of the cabin, bounding up onto the deck. Julie stood in the fading light of the dusk. He lowered the dinghy and pulled it around to the side.

"Go ashore for a few hours," he said.

"Go to hell," she retorted, arms folded across her breasts. He grabbed her arm and shoved her to the rail.

"Now listen here, doll. You got me into this damned thing in the first place. Now you do as I say and let me handle it my way."

"I know what you want to handle," she snapped angrily. "How could you? She's one of them, the ones who killed Pops. How can you even touch her?"

"I do things my way," he said. "You wouldn't understand."

"I understand you're the rottenest, lowest, stinkin' thing I've ever seen," Julie yelled at him. She was starting to say more when Logan scooped her up in one quick motion and tossed her over the side. He saw her hit the water with a resounding splash a few feet from the dinghy, and he pulled up the rope ladder on the boat's side.

"Bastard!" she yelled as she came up for air. "Rotten bastard!" He grinned for a moment as he turned after seeing her start to pull herself into the dinghy. Her fury had more in it than just anger because Doris was part of the group that had killed the old man. Part of it was plain, ordinary female jealousy. They were all jealous, even when they had no right to be.

He went down to the cabin and saw the girl sitting on the bed, clad only in white lace panties and a half-bra. Her eyes mirrored reluctance, anger, and a creeping hunger. He tore off his clothes and pulled her to him and felt her grow rigid. He pressed his lips to hers, tore the bra from her and let his hands curl around her curving, upturned breasts. Her nipples, brownish and large, sprang erect at his touch and he felt her quiver, still fighting within herself. He moved back and grinned at her and she saw it for what it was—a grin of victory—and she cried out and clawed at him. He slapped her, hard, knocking her halfway across the bed and then he was onto her, his lips pulling her breasts up into his mouth, first one, then the other, and she was crying out and protesting and opening her legs for him. Doris felt this big man's hardness against her and she grabbed his head with her hands. "Oh, God, yes, yes," she cried out, a half-scream. "Oh, God, yes!" She knew, as he moved slowly into her and she screamed in ecstasy, that she had held back too long. She felt the world moving sideways and then turning, and she was floating on a bed of unbearably sweet pain, her own body a thing beyond her command, moving beneath him, answering, wanting, craving.

Logan held the girl tightly and felt the surge of triumph as her body came to life under his savage assault. There was a wild and angry satisfaction in making love to this cold, amoral creature, in feeling his ability to make her react beyond her controlled desires. And she was beyond her carefully held control now, far beyond tossing and thrusting beneath him and crying out in long, gasping sounds, trying to free herself of the tyranny of ecstasy. She was beautiful, immaculately beautiful, with breasts that turned up at the brownish tips and quivered as he made love to her with increasing savagery. He increased his savage thrusts and she tried to hold back that last moment of capitulation, to salvage victory, and he felt her fists close to pound against his back. But he knew that if she did that, it would all have been for nothing. He would have sacrificed the very meaning of it all on the altar of pleasure. He drew back slowly, and moved forward again, alternating his every movement, using every skill at his command and suddenly he felt her body stiffen and from the depths of her there came a shriek, a wracking, shuddering shriek, and she arched her beautiful body upwards and lifted him with her.

And then it was over and she fell back onto the bed, her breath coming hard and fast. He moved from her to see her eyes on him, staring, almost dazed, unblinking. She forced them to close for a long minute and when she opened them the cool disdain was back in them. But it was tinged with something new—respect. He tossed her the white lace panties and watched her slip them on. The half-bra was torn and useless, and he let his eyes feast on the beauty of her breasts as she moved from the bed and put on the slacks. She faced him, slipping the black jersey over her head and she made no effort to disguise the victory in her eyes.

Doris studied him for a moment before saying anything. He was more than she'd expected, more in every way, and he offered more possibilities than had first entered her mind.

"After this is over I want you to look me up, Logan," she said. "We could go places together. I could use you."

"For those special occasions?" he asked and saw her eyes harden. "No, for a lot more than you ever dreamed about," she

snapped. "Play ball with me, Logan. It'll be worth your while."
Logan felt a sudden, overwhelming sadness. She was so gorgeous,
so promising. Nothing that beautiful should be that rotten. He
felt the sadness turn into the deep, furious anger at the way of the
world, the same anger that had been there from the start.

"Now where is the stuff, Logan?" Doris asked, all crisp and
contained once again.

"The old man hid it," Logan answered mildly.

"I told *you* that," Doris said with annoyance.

"So you did," Logan said, giving her a boyish smile. "That's
all I know, honey."

The small frown on Doris's brow deepened, a slow realization creeping into her eyes.

"Now wait a minute," she said. "We made a deal."

"That we did," he smiled again at her cheerfully. "I said if you
wanted to buy what I had to tell you, you knew the price. You
bought it. I told you I didn't know anything. I was only passing
along the beach when I found the old man."

Doris stood looking at him, her jaw muscles twitching, her
eyes burning with a wild rage. Logan smiled again.

"You ought to believe people more, honey," he said. "Live and
learn, eh?"

"I'll kill you," she hissed. She dived headlong across the bed,
reaching for the chair where he'd put the big Colt Python on top
of his trousers. The inside of the boat wasn't that wide, and she
had her fingers around the butt of the gun when he landed on her.
She wasn't wasting breath and energy calling him names. She
swung her arm over her head to elude his grasping hand. He got
his fingers around her wrist as she tried to bring the gun down
and felt her furious strength. She got a knee free and brought it
up against his groin, and he felt the moment's wave of pain. But
he held onto her wrist and rolled back across the bed with her,
flipping her over and landing her on the edge of the mattress.
The arena was the same and so was the struggle, essentially. He

brought her arm down hard against the wooden edge of the bed, and she cried out in pain. The Colt fell to the floor of the cabin. He yanked her up and threw her off the end of the bed. He had one big hand around her neck, pulling her out of the cabin and up the few steps to the deck. She was cursing at him now, cursing through clenched teeth as he sent her sprawling across the deck.

"Now you tell your friends that I don't know anything about this and I'm not part of it and to stay out of my hair or you haven't seen anything yet, honey," he said.

"You haven't seen anything," she hissed, getting to her feet. "You'll pay for this, you will. You can count on it."

"I always tremble like this," Logan said grimly. "Start swimming, doll."

She turned, went to the rail and dived off. It was a nice dive and her white slacks were ghostly in the dark. She cut through the water cleanly and he stood watching as her head, a blond spot in the blackness, emerged. Then, as he watched, he saw the white slacks float away on their own and, she struck out for the cruiser. It wasn't very far to swim. Besides, she could make it or she wouldn't have jumped. She wasn't the kind for gestures. He turned and went down to the cabin. He wished he felt quite as secure and confident as he'd sounded to Doris. He lay down on the bed and then, too restless to sleep, went back on deck. Taking a length of wire, he strung it around the rail of the ship, from bow to stern. Then he took out a half dozen small brass bells and hung them from the wire. It was a simple but effective alarm that had proven itself often. Leaving only the mast light on, he went back to the cabin and switched on the marine forecast. The urgent tone of the forecaster's voice told him the bad news even before he heard the words. Phyllis was still moving slowly but still heading toward the mainland and the coast. Logan said a small prayer that the hurricane would continue its slow forward movement. But you never knew with hurricanes. She could decide to pick up speed at any moment and sweep onto them like an avenging angel. The air had grown thicker and the stillness continued ominously.

Logan tried to lie still, but his skin crawled with inner tension. Then he heard the tinkle of bells. He reached over and picked up the Colt Python and moved silently to the top step of the companionway. The long blond tresses glowed softly in the dark as she moved along the rail, pulling the dinghy to the stern. He watched her tie the small boat up and then returned to the cabin. He heard her moving softly down the steps and into the forward cabin, and he smiled. Perhaps some day she might understand.

In the forward cabin, Julie Banntry undressed and lay awake, rubbing her hands down the length of her naked body, fighting down her desire to go to where Logan slept. She didn't understand him. Maybe he was all the things she'd called him. Maybe he wasn't. But whatever he was, he was beyond her. But she needed him. She could make him happy, and she felt herself stir as she thought of how he had made love to her. Pops was gone, and she had her own plans for a new life, a new world. But it was no good without someone to share it with. Anger swept over her as she thought of him with that bitch from the white cruiser. Why did he have to touch her? He must have had some good reason. But whatever it was, he'd forget about her. She'd see to that. In the morning she'd make him forget. She closed her eyes and let the gentle roll of the boat put her to sleep.

Logan still lay awake, letting certain conclusions crystallize in his mind. He was involved up to his eyeballs now. He didn't want to be, but he was. And he'd get the most out of it. Doris and her playmates weren't so determined over a set of bubble gum wrappers. Whatever they were after was valuable, very valuable. Valuable enough perhaps to provide the answer to Sister Mary Angela's letter still lying in the desk drawer. The old man had found something and had hidden it, perhaps to give himself time to think about what he should do. But they hadn't given him any time. They'd gotten to him, and perhaps he'd been stubborn. As Doris had said, "Harry got carried away" and the old man had been killed. That much was easy enough to reconstruct. But what had he found and where had he hidden it? In the old monstrosity of a house? If so, he'd have Julie go through the place with him. She was angry, he knew. And hurt. And jealous. And God knows what else. But he could handle her, spitfire that she was.

But time was running out. Doris and her friends would be getting desperate. They heard the weather reports just as he did, and they'd know that when the hurricane came, all bets would be off. And with the damn storm moving so close already he couldn't move freely, either. There would be tomorrow and that would be it. If he was to move, it had to be tomorrow. Phyllis wouldn't hold off much longer, and when she came she would descend with screaming winds and mountainous seas. He and the *Urchin* had to be somewhere else before that happened. He'd been sucked into this, maneuvered, trapped, and boxed into it. That was more than enough. He wasn't adding a hurricane to it. He forced his eyes shut and turned off his mind.

CHAPTER FOUR

It was hardly dawn, still dark with only the hint of light in the sky, when Logan heard her soft footsteps and woke at once. He lay still in the cabin and felt her move to the side of the bed and stand there, looking down at his hard-framed nakedness. Then she crawled onto the bed beside him and pressed her full breasts against his chest. He felt the lush softness of her. As she moved her breasts against him, he stirred and raised his arm to press it against the small of her back. Julie looked up at Logan and moved up to crush her lips against his. Whatever had happened last night, she would make him forget her, forget ever having had her, forget everything but what she could do to him. She moved from his lips, letting her mouth caress his cheek, down along the side of his neck and across the broad muscles of his chest. She moved her lips in a wet, sensuous path, down across his flat stomach and then, with a gasp of hunger, still further until she was making little sounds of pleasure and desire. He felt the wild flood of desire course through his body and he rose up under her to turn her over and find her rounded breasts with his mouth. Their small pink tips sprang erect, tiny, pink, as sweetly sensuous and vernal as she was. The frenzied passion of the day before was gone from her and her desires were less edged with frantic release. A full, deep, complete, and surging emotion had replaced that, even more fulfilling and more complete. She was all over his body, holding him, kissing him, stroking and straining against him.

"Oh, Logan, Logan," she said. "God, Logan, more, more." He was holding her breasts cupped in his hands, moving his lips on one, then the other, pulling and drawing them up into his mouth. Her hips twisted in desire, and she pulled at him with her hands on his buttocks. He came over to press down upon her, and she cried out and opened her full thighs in the eternal invitation of woman, and he moved to find her warm, welcoming wetness. Julie's torso rose and twisted under him as she cried out, her body urging itself on, pursuing that moment of moments, that eternal goal never reached often enough. Her hands bruising his body as she pulled them up and down along his sides, digging deeply into his skin, she began to gasp in rhythm with his movements, each gasp a grace note of ecstatic pleasure. Her lips formed words that came out only as a gasp, and suddenly she was clutched to him, her legs lifted up high around his back, moving pistonlike up and down, hanging onto him. With almost startling suddenness she let go of him and her shoulders fell back onto the bed. Then it was he who thrust deeply, over and over and her gasps rose faster and faster until there was no sound but the silent paean of pleasure beyond pleasure, of raptures never scaled before.

Julie fell limply, and Logan, staying with her, laid his body across hers, and she smiled through closed eyes. "Oh, God, Logan, it was no accident the first time," she breathed. "You're something different, all right." She opened her eyes and looked at the big man. "What is it with you?" she asked, questioning herself as much as him. "How do you make it come like you do, like it never happened before and never will again?"

He moved to lay beside her and his smile was rueful.

"Maybe because I feel just that way about it," he said. "Maybe because it's the only real thing in this damned world, the only thing nobody can change or ruin or louse up."

Her eyes were thoughtful. "Maybe it is," she said.

"Take me with you, Logan," she said and suddenly she was the waif again, that lost quality in her eyes and her voice, and he was silently amazed at how she could change from throbbing woman to little girl.

"To the first real port, remember?" he said. "You just had to get away for a little while. There were too many reminders, and you were afraid."

"I know that's what I said."

"But I meant what I said, Julie."

"I did, too, but it's different now. I know I could make it with you. I know your kind of person. And I'm not like most girls."

Logan smiled at her. "You're right there," he said. "But it's still no."

"We could try, Logan. We could try."

"It wouldn't work."

"You don't know that. There's nothing to lose. Maybe you'll be surprised."

"I don't like surprises," he grinned and ran a big hand through the long, blond hair, soft, light almost hiding his fingers in its denseness. It would be fun, he knew, for a while. For him, anyway. She was a lusty animal, a vessel of pleasure for those who could take it and not be overwhelmed by her. But it would be that and only that to him while she would want something more. It was there in her eyes already, just as she wanted him to explain his rejection of her. But she wouldn't be able to understand the only explanations he could give. She wouldn't understand that you could die and still live, that a world could shatter so completely that it left only a cold and consuming rage. She wouldn't understand that kind of a hurt, a hurt that made you see so clearly you had to look away. She hadn't lived enough yet, or loved enough. She hadn't looked deeply enough into mirrors yet. She would hate him for the uncompromising honesty he lived by. But that was the one thing he had now, the one thing he lived by, the honesty of his own hardness, of following his own trail in his own way. And no one would take that from him. Not now, not until he gave up enough of it to rejoin the world.

Besides, Julie was all emotion, a creature of the senses, not the mind. Her understanding came from her heart, not her head; her truths were felt, not reasoned. And that was all to the good, a kind of wisdom all its own and greater than most learned wisdom. But for him it would not be enough, he knew. If ever he turned to another again he would need the understanding of the mind as well as the compassion of the heart. Not a little of one and more of the other but both in full measure. And so he pushed her down on the bed and kissed her.

"It's still no, and let's drop it now," he said. "And if we don't figure out how to get rid of our friends on the cruiser you may not need to think about it again." He got to his feet and disappeared for a moment to snap on the radio. He was back beside Julie's naked warmth as the marine forecaster's voice flooded into the cabin.

"Hurricane Phyllis has picked up speed and is heading toward the Carolina coast," the announcer intoned. "It is unlikely she will change course substantially now. Her forward motion, however, is still unstable. Urgent warnings are out for all shipping. This is an extremely dangerous storm. Coastal areas should expect tides of fifteen feet or more and extreme flooding."

Logan got up and snapped off the radio. He looked at Julie and saw her face was clouded. She was standing by the porthole, looking out at the gray daylight. She reached for her clothes, frowning.

"I've got to go back to the house," she said. "I've got to get some things." Logan watched her as she dressed and saw the strange urgency in her eyes. The marine forecast had upset her deeply.

"The house is far enough back to avoid flooding, I think," he said. "And you can't do a damn thing about the wind and the waves and the rain."

"I still have to go back," she said.

"What's so important there?" Logan asked her.

"Just some things I want," she snapped. "Personal things." Evasiveness laced her irritation and Logan eyed her speculatively. She was pacing the cabin, glancing out the porthole at almost every turn.

"Some sentimental things from the old man?" he tossed out.

"Yes, that's it," she said quickly. "You think the hurricane will really hit us?" she asked him, worry in her eyes.

"You heard the man," Logan answered. He didn't want to be here then. He'd get away, head up north to that sheltered cove. This overcrowded harbor would be a graveyard for boats torn loose from their moorings. But Julie's sudden concern still bothered him. He didn't like the smell of it, and he pressed further.

"You and the old man were really close, weren't you?" he said. She nodded as she poked her head out the porthole and looked up at the sky. The first faint puffy wind was already making itself felt, blowing away the still hanging air.

"Our friends aboard the cruiser say they saw the old man find what they're after," he said casually. Julie shrugged.

"They must have seen somebody else, that's all," she replied.

"If he had found something valuable he'd have told you about it, I'd think," Logan went on. "You and he being so close and everything, no?"

"That's right," she said and suddenly there was a tinge of wariness in her voice. He didn't like it. If the scheming little bitch had been lying to him all along he'd make her sorry for it in more ways than one. He decided to press again. If his suspicions were wrong, he would have bought his answer at a damn high price. He took her by the shoulders and turned her to face him.

"Forget the house," he said. "I've been thinking about what you said. Maybe you're right about trying it, you and me. I think I can give our friends the slip. There's still time, before that damned hurricane stops us. I'm willing to give it a try."

Hope and excitement leaped into her eyes, and he felt like a heel. But then she answered.

"I can be back in a few hours," she said. "I'll go ashore and hire a car or even a cab. I can drive to Kingdom Point in just a little over an hour. I'll be back before the morning's over."

He'd gotten his answer. She wanted what he offered, all right, but something else was suddenly even more important. And the hurricane somehow figured into it. It hadn't changed her desires, just shifted around the order of priorities. She'd been willing to go off with him—hungry to—but the hurricane had loomed up to scare her. But why? If the old man had confided in her, if she knew more than she'd let on, why was the hurricane so important? If she knew what was hidden and where it was in the old house, it'd still be there, even if it was amid the rubble. The old place was back far enough to be blown down but not washed away to sea. He stepped back and smiled at her.

"If you really want to go back I guess that's it," he said. "I'll just have to wait for you. Take the dinghy. And hurry."

Her arms flew around his neck, and her lips were open and hot against his mouth. "I will," she said. "You damn well know I will."

He went on deck with her and watched her as she clambered into the dinghy, waving as she rowed off toward the docks. He stayed there till she was lost amid the welter of hulls and masts crowding the dockside. His eyes swept the small-boat owners hurriedly adding line, some letting out more mooring line, others battening down everything they could. He knew that those aboard the white cruiser had seen Julie row to shore, but he was betting they wouldn't move after her. Not so long as he hadn't gone with her. He let his eyes scan the sky. Gray, fast moving low clouds were starting to scud by and the wind was growing puffier. He turned and went below, his mouth a thin, hard line. Damn it, he cursed to himself. Time was really running out. He snapped on the weather for the latest storm advisory. They gave

Phyllis six hours to reach the coastline. Six hours and less for the gales at the perimeter of the storm. Six hours, maybe seven. Or maybe five. It wasn't much time, but it was all he had, and he had to make do with it. He cursed the blond-haired vixen for having pulled him into this in the first place. He could try to cut out now on his own and head north for that cove. But the cruiser would be after him, and he couldn't fight and steer alone, even with the automatic pilot. Besides, he had come too far to turn back now.

He took his clothes off and rolled his shirt, trousers and a towel inside a protective oilskin covering. Putting on a belt, he tied the package to it and crawled to the forward hatchway. He pushed the hatch cover up only enough to squeeze out, keeping beneath the level of the gunwale. They would have a constant watch on the *Urchin*, he was certain. But the tide had swung the bow of the boat away from the cruiser and four compass points of the port bow were out of visual range. Pushing his way across the forward deck on his stomach, almost to the bow, he reached the side of the ship. Then he slipped over the gunwale and lowered himself into the water, disappearing beneath the surface. Swimming with long, powerful strokes, he moved underwater, keeping himself in a line with the bulk of the boat. When he surfaced for a brief moment, drinking deeply of the air, he was but a tiny, bobbing spot on the water. He dived again and swam on underwater, surfacing only when his lungs were about to give out. Finally he was at the docks and pulled himself out of the water. He crouched in the shadow of a big, fifty-foot, flush-deck pleasure cruiser and unrolled the package at his waist. He dried himself with the towel, put on his clothes, and in minutes was rushing past the grim-faced, worried hordes of yachtsmen trying to prepare for the hurricane. Police cars were cruising the harbor streets with loudspeakers blaring hurricane warnings and storekeepers were attempting to shore up windows. His eyes caught a sign, *Cars For Hire,* and he hurried to the small streetfront office. The lone occupant of the office was a glum-faced, balding man.

Logan noted the black '67 Lincoln with commercial plates at the curb just outside the door.

"I want to get to Kingdom Point," he said to the man who looked up from behind the desk.

"Forget it," the man grunted. "You're the second one that's come in here wanting to go to Kingdom Point. There was a girl, little while ago."

"Where did she go?"

"I showed her where to get the bus that runs between here and the Point," he said. "She caught it. Last one running today, too."

"I'll go for anything within reason," Logan offered. The man shook his head. "I'm not risking that run now, especially back. It's all along the coastal road. I told her the same thing."

Logan grimaced. He didn't like what he had to do, but time and nature were riding him hard. He glanced out into the street, saw no one near. He whirled, striking out with a karate chop that caught the balding man on the neck. He slipped under the desk noiselessly. Logan yanked open a door. It was a broom closet. He pulled the man inside it. He found some rope and tied the man hand and foot and stuffed a makeshift gag into his mouth. Logan checked the bonds. With a little effort they'd work loose—about an hour's worth of effort.

"Sorry about this," he muttered, patting the unconscious figure on the head. He took the car keys. Seconds later he was inside the black Lincoln, heading north out of Bayville for the coastal road to Kingdom Point. His eyes swept the sky as he roared down the flat road, and he felt the pull of the gusts of wind against the car. The grayness had deepened and the low-flying clouds were hurrying. The road ran within easy view of the sea. He saw that the tides had already started to rise, and the breakers swept in with increasing speed. Traffic on the road was light, and he held the heavy car near the top of its speed, taking the gentle curves without slowing. With every glance at the sea the tide seemed to rise, the waves beginning to take on an angry hiss as they tumbled after each other. He was glad to see the low, flat buildings of Kingdom Point come into view. He threaded his way through the town, past the harbor and beyond to where the sand of the beachfront loomed before him. The road began to curve inland there and he pulled to the side and leaped from the car. A gust caught him as he started to trot along the sand. He saw the old, crumbled towers of the monstrous house rise up over the crest of sea-oats, the hardy grass screening the lower portion of it from him. He slowed and crouched. He looked for a sign of the girl inside the house. He waited, frowning at the silence. The line of windows facing the sea were open. Whatever she'd come for, she hadn't yet taken the time to close the old place. He shifted position, crawling to the side for a better view. But the empty silence persisted. "Damn!" he exploded, finally, crossing the short distance to the old house at a run. He burst in through the open door, halting in the disheveled, cluttered living room. She wasn't there. He called her name. There was no answer. But she'd been there. He saw the blouse lying on the sofa, the shorts beside it. He glanced across the rest of the room and then he saw it—the empty spot where the scuba gear had been. Eyes narrowed, he ran from the house. Between the house and the Point there was only sandy beachfront. He turned and ran north, crossing to the hard-packed sand of the beach to make better time. The wind had strengthened to a steady blow now, and the sea had risen to cover most of what ordinarily was uncovered even at high tide. The surf came rolling in hard now, each wave a curled lip of white edging the gray face of the sea behind it. And then, ahead, he saw rocks and a small inlet carved into the rock, interrupting the stretch of sandy beach. The rock rose to form a protective wall around the inlet. He clambered up it and made his way down the other side. She had to be in the waters of the inlet someplace. He stripped to his shorts, laid his clothes behind a heavy boulder, and dived into the gray, cold water. He struck out sharply, diving, and staying close to the rock, seeing it move down to become encrusted with coral.

The gathering turbulence of the surface water disappeared as he dived deeper. Then he saw her, a flash of bare legs moving close to the coral and rock. She had the air tank strapped on, and she moved slowly. Logan swam closer, moving out from the rocks. She was intent on her search, concentrating on it as she moved from rock to rock and coral to coral. She had a long pole in her right hand, and she paused at each crevice and hole to poke inside it with the pole. Without scuba gear Logan's lungs were beginning to burn, and he struck out for the surface, breaking into the air a second before they burst. He drank deeply of the air and glanced at the gray, threatening skies. The water pushed him twenty feet toward the shore in seconds, and he dived again, this time staying in the center of the little inlet. She was still intent on her search now farther along the small curve of the inlet He watched from a distance, fighting back the demand by his lungs that he surface. But she was still poking the pole into crevices when he had to kick upwards again and gasp in air. This time he drank quickly and surface-dived at once. Julie had reached a point past the center of the curve where the staghorn coral grew thick and a myriad of dark gaps clustered together. Finally she pulled at the pole and then turned, lifting a small bag from the end of the pole. It was tied at the top by a drawstring. Logan swam away quickly, striking out for the surface. He burst into the air and got a mouthful of spray, shook it out and headed for the shore, the force of the water strong enough to fling him against the rocks with bruising, scraping pain. He pulled himself out and pressed his body behind a wind-smoothed boulder.

Julie surfaced a few moments later, a dark shape fighting against the force of the water. She came ashore only a few yards from where he crouched, and he watched her slip off the air tank and rest for a moment. The little bag was tied to her wrist, and she unwound it and started to pull the drawstring open. Logan stepped from behind the boulder.

"I'll take that, Julie," he said. She gaped at him as he moved over to where she sat.

"I can explain, Logan," she said, finding her voice.

"You knew all the time," he said. "It was all an act."

"No, Logan, no it wasn't, I swear it," she said, her voice tense, tight.

"You were so upset because the old man had been killed."

"That's right, I was. Terribly upset. They didn't have to do that. I never expected anything like that."

"But you knew his death was tied into this, whatever it is," Logan countered. "I'll buy that you were shattered by it. But you knew there was a reason. You knew that all the time."

Logan felt a sadness, a hollow, empty sadness, the kind that would turn into black meanness inside him, as he fixed Julie with his deep, probing eyes. Lusty, throbbing creature, lost waif, peppery spitfire and now conniving, scheming, lying, little bitch.

"You touch all the bases, don't you?" he commented grimly.

"What do you mean?" she asked.

"You wouldn't understand," he answered. "Give me the bag."

She held back. "Will you give it back to me? Promise?" she bargained. It was a mistake. Logan wrapped his hand around the rubbery wetness of the scuba suit at her neck.

"I promise I'll twist your damn head off if you give me any more trouble," he growled. She lifted her hand and gave him the bag. She'd seen that cold hardness in his eyes once before, when he'd used the hurricane lamp on the man's face. He let her sink back onto the rocks and loosened the drawstring on the little leather sack. He dumped the contents out into his cupped palm.

"Diamonds," he said, looking at Julie. "But you knew, of course." Her sullen silence was his answer. He poured the gems back into the bag and drew the drawstring tight again. These were not raw stones but all cut and polished gems.

"You've got about fifteen seconds to tell me the truth," Logan growled. "Let's start with what I know. It was this bag of diamonds that was dropped from the low-flying plane and picked up by the old man. Take it from there."

Her eyes held his, unblinking, sad.

"Pops came home and told me what he'd found," she said. "He wanted to think about what he should do. But he hadn't wanted to bring them back to keep in the house. He was afraid someone might come looking for them and find them there. So he told me he'd hidden them, during low tide, in one of the coral crevices in the inlet, a deep one where they'd stay safe. That night we talked about right and wrong and what it would mean to be rich and not worry about tomorrow and have a lot of nice things. When Pops went to bed that night he said he didn't care much about himself, that he had the kind of riches he wanted right here. But he was thinking about what the diamonds would do for me. And the next morning they killed him."

Logan nodded. It fitted this time. The old man had no doubt been stubborn and Harry had gotten "carried away."

"I wasn't going to keep the diamonds," Julie said, getting to her feet and putting her hands on Logan's chest. "I only decided that after they killed Pops. There was nothing left for me after that, not here, not anywhere, and keeping the diamonds would at least mean he hadn't died for nothing."

"Would it?" Logan asked. "Some people would say just the opposite. Some people would say that turning them in to the cops would be the only way to show the old man hadn't died for nothing."

The stubborn thrust of her jaw grew harder.

"He would have wanted me to keep them," she said. "He would have."

"Trying to convince yourself, Julie?" Logan asked. Stubborn anger crept into her eyes. He could fit the rest of the pieces together easily now, even to the sudden fear at the news of the coming hurricane.

"You didn't want to get away from memories of the old man," he said to her. "You just wanted to get away so you could lay low safely until things cooled down. Then you'd sneak back to the inlet here and get the stuff."

She didn't answer, but she looked away, her jaw a stubborn line. It had been the hurricane that wrecked her plans. She knew that when it struck, its howling, driving fury would force churning seas into every hole and crevice in the rocks, sweeping each one clean. Her little cache would be swept away and lost forever. And as he thought of the coming storm, he turned to clamber up the rocks. Julie's arms flew around his neck.

"This hasn't changed anything, Logan," she said, anxious fear in her voice. "Only made it better for us, don't you see? I was going to tell you, later, as a surprise."

"I told you I don't like surprises," he growled and pulled away from her. "Come on."

"What are you going to do with the diamonds?" she asked.

"Nothing for now," he said. "Take them with me. There's no time for anything except getting back to the boat and finding a safe spot. And you're going with me."

He saw the pleased little glint appear in her eyes and he reached out and pulled her up to him.

"It's not for the reasons you're thinking," he said, his hand pressing hard into the soft flesh between her neck and shoulder. "If the *Urchin* and I don't make it out of this damn thing safely it'll be because of you, and you're not going to make it either then. Get that straight, Julie girl?"

"What about the things you said? ... About giving it a try?" she asked, her eyes wide.

"Bait, honey, just bait. In the same class as your story about having to get away from memories."

He let go of her and gave her a shove backwards. "Pick up the air tank and bring it along," he growled. "It might come in handy." He put on his clothes, pushed the little sack into his pocket and started up over the edge of the rocks.

"My clothes are at the house," she called after him.

"We'll pick them up. It's on the way. Your jeep still there?" She nodded. They'd use it to return to Bayville. He walked with long, hard strides, with an occasional glance to make sure the girl was close behind. They strode along the edge of the water. The sea was gray, unrelieved under a gray sky, rolling, crashing grayness, sending gray-white scud flying from the tops of the waves. The wind carried an occasional gust of rain and flung it at the two hurrying figures. Logan's grim-lipped estimate was two to three hours, not more, before the hurricane broke in full fury on them.

When they reached the old house the rain was starting to move in more forcefully, in steady, slanting sheets. Julie crossed the threshhold of the open door first, and Logan came in close behind her. He had just stepped into the huge, cluttered room when the blow struck him. With a moment of instinctive warning, he had started to duck away, but it still caught him hard enough to send him falling forward to his knees. Another blow followed it—again glancing off his head—but the room was spinning and he heard voice, and then screaming that grew dim. He a voice, a tight, hard voice, and then the girl's shook his head and kicked out with one leg, feeling his foot strike flesh and bone and hearing a cursed cry of pain. He rolled over, shook his head and the room came into focus. He got a glimpse of Doris and two men holding Julie. Then a shoe caught him in the side. Now it was his turn to gasp in pain. He rolled away, felt hands grabbing at him. He struck out with both hands, wrapping his arms around a leg and pulling. The leg's owner went over, and Logan got to one knee when another blow descended, catching him across the back of the neck. He pitched forward onto his face again. Somebody was using a billy. Darkness came over him in a wave, and he somersaulted forward, kicking both heels up and catching someone in the face. An arm tried to grab him as he landed on his back. He got hold of it, twisted and heard a satisfying groan. A foot kicked him in the side of the temple and once again the grayness descended. If only he could get on his feet. But they were all over him, not giving him a chance to spring back from that first sudden blow. He swung furiously, fighting from instinct more than anything else, bringing his blows up from the floor, rolling and kicking, punching out in all directions, feeling some land, some miss, using the powerful muscles to battle back. He heard a man cursing, shook the grayness off long enough to see two men tackle him and bring him crashing to the floor. He glimpsed others coming in and then the cold, unyielding butt of a revolver crashed down on his skull. He shook his head, but the darkness continued to wrap around him. Then there was nothing but silence and sudden sleep.

When Logan woke he felt the hard pull of the ropes tied around his wrists. He was sitting up, propped against the worn sofa, his back against the bottom portion of it, his wrists bound together in his lap. He let his eyes focus before raising his head to see the others standing in the room. Doris was nearest to him, beside the tall, cold-faced man. The man had the little sack in his hand and swung it casually by the drawstring. Julie, her wrists bound together as his were, sat against the opposite wall, still clad in the top part of her scuba suit. Doris saw Logan's head come up and turned toward him, her eyes cold.

"So you didn't know anything?" she hissed and walked over to Logan. She kicked him in the face with her pointed shoe. He turned to take the blow on the cheek and felt the trickle of blood instantly flow down his face. His legs were stretched out in front of him. He moved one, curling it around Doris's ankle and pulling hard. She went down backwards, her head hitting the wooden floor with a resounding thud. Varney quickly picked her up. She put her hand to the back of her head and winced in pain. Logan saw the others in the room, eight of them, and three starting for him.

"No," Varney said. "There's no time for that."

"Work him over, boys," Doris said. "Work him over till the bastard's face looks like Harry's did."

"I said no," Varney spoke up. "We'll fix them up and get out of here." As if to add emphasis to his words, the wind tore a shutter from the window and sent it clattering along the side of the house.

"Damn it, Varney," she snapped. "Maybe you better just do what I say without arguing all the time. You argued about coming here, too."

The man's eyes narrowed. "Shut up, Doris," he said. "So you were right. But I'm still running this show."

There was trouble simmering just below the surface. Maybe it could be fanned. Maybe a fight amongst them would give him a break, a chance. All maybes but what the hell, he had nothing to lose at this point. He shot Julie a glance which told her to keep her mouth shut. He hoped she got the message. Her eyes were sullen, defiant. The rest of the men watched Varney and Doris.

"You better listen to Doris," Logan said. "It seems Doris gives good advice."

Varney turned to look at Logan. "She thought things were too damned quiet on your boat after the girl left," he said. "We didn't see you anywhere, not even stirring around below decks."

"And so Doris said you'd better get the hell back here to the house," Logan finished. "I told you, Doris is smart. She gives everyone good advice. You ought to know the offer she gave me."

Varney turned to face Logan more fully.

"What offer?" he said.

"She offered me a big piece of your operation," Logan said, smiling up at Varney. "In fact, she said she could use me as a replacement."

"Varney! Are you going to listen to that lying sonofabitch?"

It was Doris, her voice sharp and commanding. The tall man looked at her, a slow, icy look. "Shut up, Doris," he said softly. "Let's hear what he has to say."

Doris was white-faced, her eyes blazing. "He's lying, don't you see that?"

"Am I, Doris?" Logan laughed, his mind racing on. He thought of the diamonds in the sack, all cut and polished, finished pieces. He threw out an educated guess.

"That's why I knew you've got a fancy operation," he said. "An operation that needs Doris to front it. That's why I know I could be fitted into it."

Varney was looking at Doris as he spoke to Logan.

"Who were you thinking of replacing with him, Doris?" he said. "You weren't going to use him to go into the jewelers and buy the pieces, were you? No, that's your job. And you weren't thinking about him bringing the pieces back to them after he switched stones, were you? No, not that, either. You have to carry through on that. Who were you going to replace with him, baby?"

"Nobody," Doris said, but there was fear in her eyes, fear that revealed guilt. Varney saw it, too. With a suddenness that surprised Logan, he struck Doris across the face. It made her head twist, and she staggered backwards.

"He's lying," Doris gasped out. "Look, Varney, believe me." Her eyes were wide and fearful and she moved to the tall cold-faced man. "You wanted something from me, Varney," she said. "You'll get it. Everything you wanted. He's lying, I tell you."

Logan was seeing the whole picture, now, putting it together. It was a smooth, sophisticated operation, all right. Varney's few questions had revealed it in broad strokes. Doris was sent into jewelry stores in rich, swank communities with a good check to purchase a particular piece on approval of a nonexistent husband or boyfriend. It was a common enough practice. They took a few days, maybe a week, to switch the diamonds in the piece with fakes, probably undetectable by the ordinary jeweler's glasses. Then she brought the piece back, saying it was not liked by the husband, got her check back and they took off with the real stones.

Logan looked up to see Varney staring coldly at him. The old house suddenly creaked and groaned in a hard gust of wind. "Let's get out of here, Varney," Doris said. "Just kill them and let's go."

"We'll do it the way I said we would," Varney answered. "Plain old murders bring cops and cops bring questions and questions bring searches. That's why we ditched the old man, remember?" He gestured to three of the others. The men pulled Julie to her feet and threw her down beside Logan. "We'll let the hurricane do the dirty work for us," Varney smiled. The others seized Logan and rolled him against Julie, back to back, and tied ropes around them both, binding them together, pinning their arms tight in front of each of them. In a few moments they were tightly bound, unable to move more than their toes.

"Get them down to the water," Varney said. "If they're ever found when the hurricane blows over it'll look like whatever they tried to do just went wrong someplace. People do all sorts of crazy things at times like this."

Four of the men half lifted, half dragged them out into the rain and the wind, dragged them across the wet sand. He could see Doris walking along beside him, and he saw the racing clouds overhead, all dark gray, moving with the impatience of waiting death. The taste of salt water mingled with the rain now. They were at the edge of the rising, roaring sea. The men threw them forward, into the leading edge of the sea, and a wave immediately flung itself over them. When it had receded, he saw the others walking away. Only Doris hung back for a moment, cold victory in her eyes, a special victory only he and she knew about. The wind rose, curled around them and threw the sea over them. Their bodies shook in the force of the breaking waves and he heard Julie coughing out salt water.

"Use your breath as if you were swimming," Logan called. The water broke over them again and they were half in the sea, now, being moved by the swirling surf. Julie coughed and sputtered, and he felt the movement of her back muscles.

"Watch your breath," he called again. "Try to time it with the waves."

"It's no use," Julie coughed. "I'm sorry, Logan, I am."

"That makes two of us," Logan answered bitterly. The sea struck him in the face, but he held his breath as the water flowed over and around him and then receded. But another wave followed at once and he had chance for only a short breath. It wouldn't take long, he knew. They'd be engulfed in a matter of minutes, swept in on the fierce, roaring waters and then out again. Goddamn it, Logan swore. No, it wouldn't end this way. Not without a final try. He wasn't ready to cash it all in yet. There were too many unfinished things to do—one especially. His anger at the world exploded, and it took in the girl strapped against him, the vicious amoral creature from the white cruiser, and himself. He twisted and pulled his arms, crying out in pain, but the wet ropes refused to budge. A huge wave came in, and he felt himself lifted, sent swirling and rolling by it, his body riding up over Julie's, and then her body across his as the sea rolled them along. As the waters receded he yelled. "Roll over. Dig your feet in. Push and roll."

"What?" Julie sputtered back.

"Roll, damn it," Logan yelled again. He pushed his feet in against the wet sand as the waves struck him again, and he rolled over the girl. "Now you do it," he velled, and he felt her push her body and rise, rolling over with him.

"Keep it up," he yelled. "Keep going. All the way to the house."

The girl rolled over him again and then he rolled over her and they rolled and tumbled together like some unearthly insect and finally she gasped out in pain.

"I can't, Logan," she said. "I can't anymore."

He kicked out savagely, as hard as his bonds would permit him, and rolled over her. He pulled at her with his powerful shoulder muscles. "Come on, damn you," he yelled. "Come on."

He felt her back arch and she came over again. The old house loomed up in the driving rain. "Just a little farther," Logan called to her. Once more he pressed his shoulders up and started her over. She was crying as she came over and crashed to the ground. His body rolled over hers, and she continued crying, great, gasping sobs of pain and weariness as they reached the doorway and pushed their way inside. His own body ached and throbbed, but the cold, bitter anger inside him carried him on. Julie screamed in pain as he rolled over her on the wood of the floor and came to rest against the doorway leading to the kitchen. He saw the handle of the bread knife hanging off the edge of the shelf and kicked at the wood of the kitchen cabinet. The knife shivered, and he kicked again. It fell to the floor. He rolled, pulling Julie with him, and got his hands on the handle. Turning back, he lay on his side and pressed the knife against the ropes that encircled them, sawing it back and forth, each motion traveling no more than an inch. But the knife was sharp and it cut through the cord, little by little, the strands parting with agonizing slowness. Logan listened to the old house shudder as the wind rose still higher, and he wondered if he were not already too late. But he continued to saw against the rope, cursing under his breath with every movement of the bread knife and then, suddenly, it came apart in a small shower of twine. The ropes binding them together loosened and he struggled free, kicking himself away from Julie. The knife still in his hands, the angle too sharp to reach the ropes binding his own wrist, he moved to the girl and cut her wrist bonds. She sat up, breathing hard, her face still echoing the pain of her body, and untied his wrist ropes.

He was on his feet instantly, pulling her up. With one hand he scooped up the air tank as he ran into the living room. "My clothes," Julie cried.

"No time," Logan answered. Outside, the wind and the rain struck them with an angry hand, pushing them against the house. The jeep was around at the rear, and he threw the air tank in the back and leaped in. The winds were a raging gale now, and he peered through the driving rain at the low-flying clouds as he sent the jeep roaring away from the old house. Another hour and a half, perhaps, before Hurricane Phyllis hit with all her fury.

His eyes were bitter and cold as they roared through the gale winds of the perimeter of the storm. He was seeing the harbor at Bayville in his mind, thinking about the *Sea Urchin* as she waited there for them. He saw the ships straining at their moorings, saw the carnage of those too tightly tied to the docks, and he pressed the gas pedal to the floor. They roared away from the sand and onto the road to Kingdom Point. He looked over at Julie huddled in the front seat, but the terror and fear in her didn't touch him at all. The hurricane of bitter anger raging inside him could match anything that happened outside. They would pay, the girl, the cold-faced man, the whole lot of them. And if the *Urchin* were lost, Julie would pay, too.

CHAPTER FIVE

Logan kept the gas pedal to the floor as they careened through the deserted streets of Kingdom Point, and he briefly wondered if Jennifer and the boy had found safe shelter. He sent the jeep spinning onto the coastal road to Bayville. His fingers were cramped and stiff from gripping the wheel so tightly. He glanced at Julie, and saw her swaying despite her grip on the edge of the seat.

"You'll fall out sitting up here," he said. "Get down on the floor and wedge yourself against the seat." Julie, fear making her obedient, slid down to crouch on the floor, braced against the bottom of the seat. The wind and the rain tore at the jeep as Logan sent the small, open vehicle roaring along the road. But it was not the wind or the rain that reached the deadliest hands for them. The sea sent its fury rolling inland to obliterate the road in spots with a frenzy of leaping waves. He took a curve, skidding through it, when suddenly there was no road in front of him, only the sea, straining further inland. He peered ahead and saw the road where the land rose. Taking aim at the road on the other side of the raging sea, he sent the jeep ahead, hoping there were no unseen curves beneath the sea. A wave crashed against the side of the jeep, sending it skittering sideways and out of control. As his shoulder muscles cried out in protest, he fought the wheel and felt the tires cling to the road while the sea smashed into them again, waist-high, dousing Julie completely where she sat on the floor. But the vehicle continued to move forward as he kept her going in reckless, unstinting speed until the ground rose and carried them up beyond the sea's reach. They sped along a stretch of road where only the wind and the rain grabbed at them, and then down into another sea-covered portion. With every passing minute the wind heightened and the sea took away more sections of the road. But with every minute they drew closer to Bayville. Finally Logan saw the tall tower of the church through the grayness and the rain.

Once more they roared through a ghost town of rain-swept streets and boarded storefronts, skidding to a halt at the edge of the harbor. The wind had whipped the harbor into a churning froth and the smaller boats foolishly made tight to the docks were already being lifted over and smashed against the quays. Dimly, through the downpour, he could see the *Urchin*. He was grateful she was farthest out in the harbor, free of the danger from boats torn loose of their moorings and driven toward shore. And the white cruiser was still there, straining hard at its anchor line. But he knew it would be, as he knew they'd be aboard, huddled inside, trying to sit out the storm. He felt Julie's eyes on him and turned to the girl.

"We can't go out there," she said. "Nobody can. It would be suicide. A boat would be turned over in seconds. A swimmer would be broken to pieces against the docks."

"Put on your air tank," Logan answered flatly. Even the pelting rain could not hide the sullen anger of her eyes.

"Dive in and down," Logan said. "With your scuba gear you can get far enough below the surface turbulence."

"Then what?"

"Take a visual bearing on the white cruiser now," he commanded. "Look at it and swim out to it underwater. When you get there, hang onto the anchor line and wait for me."

Julie saw the cold determination in the big man's rain-soaked face, the unswerving line of his jaw. There was no fear of failure there, no concession to reason in those eyes.

"What are you going to do?" she asked.

"Pay back our friends," he growled. "Get those stones back."

"They're not that important to me, Logan," Julie said.

"Who the hell cares about you?" he shot back. "They are to me now. They've tried to kill me three times. They'll keep trying if I let them. It's too late to turn back now. I'm finishing it once and for all."

He pushed Julie forward and lifted the air tank up, strapping it onto her back, holding her against a fierce gust of wind that pushed her sideways. He moved to the edge of the nearest dock as a wave smashed against it and threw its spray fifteen feet into the air. They huddled together for a moment as the front of the dock exploded in a shower of flying bits of wood.

"All right—now!" he yelled in her ear, running forward with her, throwing her into the churning waters. He knelt for a moment, watching her black-suited form disappear under the surface. Then he was engulfed in a cascade of water that knocked him down and carried him back along the dock. He felt himself crash into the side edge of the pier and felt his body shake from the force of the blow. But he crawled forward as the wave spent itself, waited for a moment to see another huge wave gathering itself, and then ran for the end of the dock. He went off in a running dive, beating the towering wave by seconds, knifing through the water, striking out downwards, fighting his way to the calmer depths below. Somewhere ahead of him Julie was swimming toward the cruiser. He leveled off and struck out in the same direction. He swam with powerful strokes, making as much headway as he could while his lungs held out. He'd have to surface for air and each time he'd lose some of the precious distance he'd make. He kept swimming, fighting off the protest of his lungs until his chest felt as though it would burst. Finally he struck out for the surface, buffeted by the water as he neared the top. He was flung up and into the air, gulping in great draughts of oxygen as the waves swept him backwards, lifting him in huge watery hands. Gauging, waiting, he let himself be scooped up by a wave and then, as it rose, he surfaced-dived and avoided being swept away by the crest. But he had lost precious distance, and he struck out below the surface again, covering what he'd lost and half again as much before he had to come up again. Time and again the exhausting procedure was repeated and time and again the surface fury swept away half of what he'd gained below.

But he managed to avoid being tossed to his death on a breaking crest each time, and each time he swam a little further underwater until he saw the cruiser's hull ahead. He made out the dark figure of Julie, clinging to the anchor line in her scuba suit. He passed behind her and went around to the starboard side of the vessel, now fighting against the churning water. He moved about fifty feet beyond the cruiser before surfacing. As he burst onto the surface he was immediately seized and swept along by the fury of the water toward the white-hulled cruiser. The vessel was tossing and heaving in the waves, and he saw they'd left the side ladder out. He'd counted on that kind of sloppy seamanship from them, and he smiled. Another high, driving wave lifted him up. He rode it high and then down into the trough, then up again. He saw it was no good. He'd be on the crest when he reached the cruiser. He surface-dived into the rising crest, knifing through it as it broke over him and found himself out on the back side of it, being seized by another wave immediately. This one, with the few seconds difference in time, carried him down into its trough as it rolled beneath the cruiser. He reached out, getting his hand onto the ladder along the boat's side, tightening his grip on it at once, and feeling the wave pulling his arms out of their sockets as it tore at him. But he clung to the ladder, and the boat carried him up and out of the sea's grip for a moment as it rose on still another wave. He locked a leg around the ladder and started to climb up. The wind helped push him over the rail, onto the deck. He felt himself sliding along the wet deck, coming to rest against the side of the cabin. Grabbing a door handle, he pulled himself to his feet. The motor cruiser was pitching terribly, but he got the door open and fell into the enclosed corridor. He lay there on the floor and let his breath come back. Finally, he got to his feet, pressing close to the outside wall of the cabin as the cruiser rolled violently. He peered into a window and saw a man with curly black hair, holding a whiskey bottle in one hand, trying to gauge the roll of the ship as he lifted the bottle to his lips.

Logan moved fast, flinging open the door and diving into the room. Tackling the man, they both went flying into a corner of the cabin as the vessel rolled hard to port. The bottle rolled from the man's grip to the floor and Logan seized it, smashed it apart against the wall molding and held the jagged end to the man's throat. Stark fear was in the man's eyes. The ship rolled, and the glass nicked his throat. "Where are the diamonds?" Logan growled at him.

"Varney has them, in the main stateroom, amidships," the man blurted out. Logan pulled him to his feet, spun him around and got an arm across his neck. He pushed him out the door and onto the deck. The man tried to twist away, but Logan's grip was viselike.

"I can't swim!" he screamed. Logan put his shoulder into the man's back and pushed. The man hit the rail and went over, his scream lost in the howl of the wind. Logan took a moment to glance at the sky and feel the wind slam him back against the cabin. Phyllis was on them with fury—but not quite full yet. He gave himself another fifteen minutes Moving back into the inside corridor, he made his way along it, passing cabin windows quickly, glimpsing the men inside them. The main stateroom of the cruiser had curtained windows. Varney was in there, the man had said. But who else? And how many? He'd passed cabins with four or five men inside them. That still left at least three besides Varney and Doris. But there was no time for caution any longer. There never had been. He stepped back and hit the door with a shattering dive. It flew open, and he pitched into the room. Doris was there, and Varney, and a third man, one of the two ex-pugs.

Doris looked at the soaked, wild-eyed figure in open-mouthed astonishment. The ex-pug, slow to react normally, was even slower now. Logan took him out with one roundhouse punch that caught him on the jaw. He crashed back against the table in the center of the room and fell to the floor. Varney reacted fast, pulling a .38 from his jacket pocket. He fired just as the boat pitched sharply, this time to starboard, and the shot went into the corner of the cabin. Logan dived for him, catching him at the knees and bringing him down. His second shot hit the ceiling as he fell. Logan had an arm on his throat, pressing hard. Varney's eyes started to bulge.

"The diamonds! Where are they?" Logan spat out. Varney moved his left hand, slapping it against his trouser pocket. Logan crossed a short right to his jaw, and the man's eyes rolled upward and closed. He pulled at the trouser pocket and yanked out the little sack. A sound behind him made him dive forward flat, across Varney's limp form, and a wooden chair smashed into his back. The ship pitched again, and he rolled over, tossing the chair aside to see Doris, fighting to keep her balance and stay on her feet. But Doris was the least of the problems. Varney's two shots had brought the others. They tumbled into the stateroom from the port door. Logan saw there was a starboard door. He dived for it, yanked it open as another shot rang out, splintering the wood less than an inch from his head as he raced through the doorway. Tying the sack around his wrist with the drawstring as he ran, he dived over the rail of the cruiser, the wind catching his body and tossing him into the sea. He landed on his back and took a deep breath as he was flung sideways, then turned in a somersault. He came out of the somersault, found a moment between waves, and surface-dived. Once more he fought his way below the turbulence which reached deeper now.

Julie's dark shape emerged as he swam to the anchor line. He moved to her, handed her the little sack and waved her forward, pointing in the direction of the *Sea Urchin*. She nodded, and he clung to her back as she started off, letting her pull him along, conserving his breath and strength. They'd made up a little less than halfway to the *Urchin* when he felt his breath going and left the girl to strike out for the surface. He came out and once more was flung about helplessly. His legs were hardly more than hanging appendages, with little muscle strength left in them, his arms aching and ready to fall off. He concentrated on getting in enough air for another dive, and he let himself be tossed by the angry waves. He knew that he survived only because the water was harbor water, angry hurricane driven, but still harbor water, broken up by the mouth of the area. Outside there was the real fury of the sea, the real pounding of the water driven unchecked across hundreds of miles. He gathered his little remaining strength and surface-dived again, taking in a glimpse of the *Urchin's* position as he did. Getting below the turbulence took more time and used up more strength, but he kept going. The *Urchin's* hull loomed up before him and he saw Julie clinging to the anchor line. He motioned to her to follow him, and he grasped the line and pulled himself up it. As he broke into the air he wrapped both legs around the anchor line and pulled himself up it. The sea and the wind tore at him, trying to dislodge him, but he clung to it like a spider clinging to the strands of its web. He inched his way up to the bow of the *Urchin,* each moment's progress a battle to hang on against the waves that swept over him, pulling and tearing at him. At the bow of the boat he grasped the gunwale and let the wave that burst over him catapult him onto the deck. He untied a line wound around a cleat and threw it to Julie as she clung to the anchor rope. She could never pull herself up it as he had, he knew. She grabbed the line and swung free with the sea pulling at her, pushing her out. Bracing himself against the wooden rail, Logan began to pull her in, his back muscles tearing and screaming in pain. But he pulled and finally she was against the hull, being slammed into it by the waves. She had slipped off the air tank. He pulled her up. As her blond hair came level with the top of the gunwale, he grabbed her, and they both toppled to the deck as the boat pitched to port. She lay there, her breath coming in great gasps.

"Into the pilot house," he said to her. She shook her head and lay there. "I can't move," she said. Logan kicked her in the rump, turning her over. "Into the pilot house," he yelled again. "Crawl in and stay there."

Logan crawled to the small forward mast where a rail held a small hand axe. He took the axe and crawled back to the anchor line. Five hard blows severed the line, and the boat immediately rose on the crest of a wave and went scooting forward. Logan crawled and stumbled his way to the pilot house, falling into the protected dryness of the cabin. Fighting off the nausea of exhaustion, he pulled himself up on the wheel seat and switched on the engines. Julie, huddled in a corner, watched him with disbelieving eyes.

CHAPTER SIX

Aboard the white cruiser as it pitched and rolled dangerously, Varney and Doris made their way to the deck, clinging to a lifeline they'd rigged up and tied around themselves. The other men held onto the line from inside the cabin.

"Shut up, Doris," Varney said to the girl as she continued to loose a string of curses. "I didn't expect to see the crazy bastard any more than you did. So we'll get the stuff back from him when the storm's over. He can't go anywhere till then."

Doris peered through the rain and the wind and the spray of the leaping sea, and her eyes darkened in disbelief.

"No?" she cried out. "He can't go anywhere, you goddamned fool? Look out there."

Varney peered through the rain. "He's moving!" the man exclaimed, awe in his voice. "He's heading out to sea."

Doris's face was a mask of fury. "Get the engines started," she screamed at Varney. "Follow him. He's not going to get away." She turned and looked out at the *Sea Urchin* moving slowly toward the mouth of the harbor. He wasn't going to win, she told herself through gritted teeth. The big, mean, no-good bastard wasn't going to win. She remembered his body against hers, his complete and utter victory over her in bed, and the way she had wanted and hated him all at once. And she remembered how he'd laughed at her afterwards.

"Goddamn it, get going," she screamed. Varney watched the other boat in transfixed awe.

"It's suicide," Varney protested. "Going out there is suicide."

"You sniveling sonofabitch," Doris shouted at him. "If he can do it so can we. He's not about to commit suicide, not that big bastard. He's too mean to do that."

Varney looked at Doris's hate-filled face. Then he turned and called into the cabin. "We're going after him," he said. "Get started. Make it fast." He turned to look at the girl again. She'd been right about damn near everything so far in this messed-up affair. Maybe she was right about this. The white-hulled cruiser shuddered to life and one of the men went forward to cut the anchor line. The vessel turned, rolling terribly as she did, and her propellers churned the water as she took after the *Sea Urchin.*

Aboard the *Urchin,* Julie peered through the rain smeared glass of the pilot-house windows and saw the motor cruiser swing around to follow after them.

"They're coming," she cried out to Logan as he wrestled with the ship's wheel. "They're coming after us."

He smiled, a slow smile of satisfaction. "I figured as much," he said quietly, and Julie shook her head. Logan steered the boat through the harbor's mouth and into the sea. There'd be no chance to reach the cove up to the north, but there was another only a few miles down. It was high-walled, protected, but with a narrow entrance. It would have to do. There was nothing else. The first wave of the open sea caught the boat, lifting it up and plunging it down, down, down into a trough so deep Julie saw nothing but walls of water all around them. She screamed in terror, but they rose again. They were still there, still afloat. Logan was turning and twisting the wheel, meeting each roaring wave with the bow, heading out into the wild fury of the hurricane. He would have to turn for the cove, he knew, but he would head in at an angle for it. Gray-green mountains of water rose to tower over them and sweep them up in a rush. A powerful wave caught them four points off the starboard bow, and Julie felt the boat shudder and seem to halt for a moment. She heeled over but came back at once, and Logan sent her forward again.

And now Julie began to realize the power and seaworthiness of the *Urchin*, the strength and balance built into her. A tremendous wave caught them, carried them up and sideways and half around. They were struck amidships. Julie crashed against the back wall of the pilot house. A window shattered. The boat quivered and her seams cried out but she came back and Logan managed to head her into the wind again. Julie glanced back and she saw the white shape against the gray water, pitching and rolling from side to side.

Aboard the cruiser, Varney stood ashen-faced beside Doris. He heard the sea slam into the boat, heard the sound of wood being pounded to pieces. A wave swept over the entire vessel, and he saw the port rail break away and fall into the furious waters. The man stood beside the girl at the pilot-house window, and two helmsmen struggled with the wheel. The boat was a bucking bronco, nosing into the sea and shuddering each time, coming up to be slammed sideways. One of the doors to the enclosed cabin was flung open and a man fell inside.

"She's leaking below decks," he gasped. "The port side has sprung. Turn back."

"No!" Doris screamed. "Not till he does."

"Turn back," Varney said to the helmsman. The man started to turn the wheel when a mountain of roaring water swept over them and the sound of splintering wood and crashing glass fought through the storm. The white hull shuddered and wallowed and the sounds of men screaming carried into the cabin. A figure burst in again. "The seams have split," he yelled. We're going down."

Varney turned to Doris. He hit her in the jaw, and she flew across the cabin and into the man at the wheel, bounced off him and fell to the floor. She lay there, dazed.

"Bitch!" Varney spat at her. He grabbed at the ship's wheel with the helmsman, frantically spinning it. But the cruiser hardly responded as the hole widened and the water poured through the seams. She was heeling fast, her stern already under water on the port side.

"They're sinking," Julie cried out inside the *Urchin's* cabin. "Their boat's coming apart."

Logan nodded, and Julie stared at him. "You know that would happen, didn't you?" she said. "You knew they'd follow you and their boat could never take these seas. You figured to get them all at once this way."

Logan didn't answer, but he glanced back at the white hull. It was going down, starting to turn on its side. He watched a huge wave lift them up and pass and then they were in a wide trough.

He spun the wheel and they turned before the next one caught them. He headed back toward the coastline, angling the *Urchin* for the little cove south of Bayville. They were alone in the raging storm now, driving before a sea of destruction. He kept checking in back of him, letting the boat ride the waves as they caught up to him and rolled on with gargantuan power. The *Urchin's* seams were shuddering, too, he felt, but she'd been built for seaworthiness, constructed to withstand the elements. She was no thin-skinned pleasure boat designed and built for smooth water. But a hurricane was something beyond ordinary power. She could stand a lot, but hurricanes had taken down huge liners. It would have taken them but for the fact that they could ride over most of the waves. It war only every sixth or seventh one that really smashed into them.

"Are we going to make it?" Julie asked, her voice tremulous. Logan shrugged. The line of the shore was coming into view and the fury of the storm had them in its grip. He gunned the engines to ride a towering wave and then slacked power to let it carry them down into its trough. He felt his body clammy with cold perspiration, his muscles tiring fast. His shoulders ached from holding the wheel against the sea's efforts to wrestle it from him. The rain slackened slightly as the eye of the hurricane was approaching. There'd be a few minutes' relative calm before the back of the storm delivered the one-two punch that was part of a hurricane's deadliness. The little cove jutted out from the coastline, high walls of rock surrounding it. But the tide was so high that the rocks that jutted out toward the center from each side were below water. He maneuvered the *Urchin,* angling the bow for the far line of the rocks. A wave lifted them and flung them sideways on its back, and then another, like the coils of some monstrous sea serpent rising up beneath them. Logan kept the bow pointed toward the far end of the rocks. Suddenly the rain stopped, and he could see more clearly. They were nearing the center of the entrance. He pushed the throttle to full and sent the boat churning forward. The sea seized them, lifting and pushing them sideways again. Logan's lips were a tight line, and Julie saw the tension in his face. The rocks stretched out from both sides, soomewhere beneath that churning, foam-flecked water. He had to be exactly in center to make it, even on the calmest of days. It was like threading a needle with the boat the thread. It would take more than skill, now, he knew. It would take luck. It would take a smile from fate, a reward for having fought a good fight.

They were moving toward the line of rocks on the top of the thrusting waves, almost broadside. Suddenly Logan saw that they were too far off center. He gunned the powerful engines, but the propellers caught only part of the sea as a wave lifted them on its head. He held his breath.

"Get ready to jump," he said to Julie. "Get by the door." The line of the rocks was just ahead, and he was helpless to do anything but hold the wheel and keep her from slipping further off center. They were abreast of the rocks, and then they were in the little cove, past the line of the rocks. The tide had risen high enough to sweep them over the rocks. Ordinarily, their position would have sent them crashing into oblivion. Inside the cove, he headed the *Urchin* for the left edge, behind the sheltering wall. He cut the engines just enough to maintain headway against the pitch of the water.

"Hold the wheel where she is," he told Julie and brushed past her to the deck. He had an emergency anchor which he dragged to the bow and dropped over the side. It was smaller than the regular one, but it would hold in the shelter of the cove. He felt the anchor line grow taut as the anchor caught on the bottom, and he went back to the pilot-house. He cut off the engines and stood quietly, leaning against the wheel, his head bowed low. The thunder of the sea crashing against the rocks outside the little cove was a kind of victory hymn. But he didn't really feel victorious. He felt terribly tired and strangely sad and still angry.

He looked across at the girl whose long blond hair was still tight and wet against her head. She had nearly cost him his boat and his life. He turned, opened the door of the pilot-house and stumbled down to the aft cabin. He flung himself on the bed, face down, and his body shuddered with complete exhaustion. His stomach was a tight knot and everything was suddenly all so very far away, almost as in a dream. His eyes closed, and he was wrapped quickly in the blanket of complete exhaustion.

Julie stayed in the pilot-house for a moment longer then slowly went below. She passed the inert form stretched face down across the bed and went into the forward cabin. She took off the top of the scuba suit and lay down, pressing her breasts into the softness of the bed. She turned over and ran her hands down her body and smiled. It was unbelievable but she was here, alive. Every muscle burned with pain, but she was alive. And Logan was alive with her. And the diamonds were in their hands. She closed her eyes. In the morning, she'd make him see. In the morning, he would feel differently.

The wind still howled and the sea still crashed against the rocks beyond the cove. But the terror was gone from it now. She and the big man were together, alive. They'd made it. He'd realize it meant something more than just their survival. She was still smiling as she fell off to sleep.

CHAPTER SEVEN

The sun was shining warmly when Julie opened her eyes in the morning. She lay still and listened to the gentle slap of the water against the hull. Yesterday's fury and terror was dreamlike, only she knew better. She got up, naked, and peered out of the porthole at the soft blue of the water. She shivered as she thought of the gray, angry awesomeness of the sea yesterday. But then that was the sea, always its own master, gentle lover and screaming killer. She smiled as she thought of the man in the aft cabin. It was a description that fitted him, too. She thought of how he had made love to her, and she thought of the coldness of his smile as the white cruiser disintegrated in the pounding seas. But loving or cruel, he was something special, something she would make hers.

On silent bare feet she crept into the cabin. During the night sometime he'd stripped off his shorts, and he lay naked on the bed, his powerful frame a thing of lithe beauty. His torso had twisted so that he lay half on his side. She went over to him, pressing her fingers into his back, massaging the rippling muscles with her hands. Logan stirred and felt the strength of the girl's fingers as they moved up and down his back. Then they crept across his ribcage, and he turned on his back to see her, her long blond hair now dry and full framing her face like a halo. Her full lips were half open as she ran her hands across his chest, and he watched her breasts rise and fall in a steady rhythm. There was something different in her touch this time. She moved her body against his and he felt his skin come alive. He reached down and pulled her across his body and took her deep, rounded breasts and stroked them.

"Oh, Logan, Logan," Julie cried out, the throbbing, sensuous Julie. He leaned down and took one full breast in his mouth, pulling at it, holding it, moving his tongue across it, and her body was working itself up and down in frenzied pleasure. She pressed her breast deeper into his mouth, wanting to have it all, wanting to become part of him and when he pulled away she cried out and clutched him to her. He rolled over on her and caressed the full-fleshed curves of her body, cupping the deep breasts, playing on the slight convexity of her belly. "I want you, Logan, I want you," she breathed, her breasts against his chest. He moved his hand across her torso and held her with a gentle motion. Her body began to move, slowly at first, undulating rhythmically. Logan held her tighter and her breath came in gasps. She cried out, and he bore down on her as her cries grew louder. She was clutching at him, now, and her lips moving across his chest and shoulders as he carried her higher and higher. And then, as it seemed she would reach new peaks of ecstasy, he pulled away from her and rolled to the side.

"Oh, my God, no!" she screamed and sprang upon him, a feverish, pleading, wanting tigress, and he grinned at her and came to her again, carrying her up once more, only now it was all the greater for the interruption. Her body was building its own crescendo and once again she heard the thunder of the seas crashing against the rocks—only now the hurricane was all inside her, whirling and roaring. "Logan, Logan, oh my God, Logan," she gasped and sank down upon the bed. He moved in her, and she came instantly alive again, wanting more. He gave her more, and it was like no other time. There was more of everything, more of her hunger, more of his own desires. She had to give all that was in her, holding nothing back, for to her, it was a beginning. He wanted to give all he could to her, for he knew it was an ending.

The throbbing, sensuous creature he'd seen that first day on the beach was beyond stopping until finally, with steady, mounting ecstasy, he made the sea stop moving for an instant and the sun explode inside her quivering body. Then she fell back and lay still, spent, satisfied. He moved beside her and let his eyes feast on her beauty, the complete womanly magnificence of her body. They lay side by side for a spell, their bodies touching, the lingering warmth of their passions translated into tactile sensations. She turned and lifted herself onto his chest. Her eyes were clear.

"Oh, Logan, it's so perfect," she said to him. "Just the two of us, together. It was meant to be that way. That's why we lived through yesterday."

Logan smiled. The throbbing sensuous creature had given way to the wide-eyed romantic girl.

"Yesterday isn't finished," he said. "Don't cast it away so quickly."

"Oh but it is," she said, pulling herself up on one elbow, her breasts just barely touching his skin, their rounded undersides lightly resting against his chest. God, he could take her again, he realized. But there had to be an end to it. There had to be or she'd win in her own way.

"All the bad part of yesterday is done with, Logan," she said. "Only the good things are left."

"Like what?"

"You. Me."

"And the diamonds," he finished for her. She nodded. "Julie, honey," he said softly. "It's still the first real port for you. That's still where you get off."

She frowned and threw herself down on his chest again.

"Not anymore, Logan, there's no need for that now," she said, the eager, happy child again, simple and terribly appealing, shifting from one flashing mood to another like quicksilver. "We can do what we want, go where we want, have whatever we want," she said, getting up on her elbow again, using her beauty with complete naturalness, fighting with it without even know-ing she was.

"I do that now, Julie," he reminded her. "It still wouldn't work. I told you that once already."

"But it will work, Logan," she pouted. "Especially now."

"But the diamonds are going back, honey," he said. "To the police."

Her eyes darkened, and her pout grew more pronounced.

"No," she said, the edge of stubbornness creeping into ther voice. "Not after all that's happened. It just wouldn't be right. We've earned them."

Logan grinned at her. She could supply her own excuses with the same speed that she could change moods.

"You know better than that," he said. She put her hands on his chest, all eager sincerity.

"They probably couldn't even be traced back to anyone, Logan," she countered. "It'd be just a big waste of everything. They'll rot away in some lockbox."

"Diamonds don't rot away," he grinned at her. "And these certainly won't. Once the police learn how the operation worked they'll send a bulletin to all jewelers. The jewelers will have their major pieces analzyed and the ones with the phony stones will come forward. It'll work out."

She was watching him with a frown, her eyes angry and defi-ant. He swung himself from the bed.

"I'll make breakfast," he said. "We can take our time sailing back to Kingdom Point."

"You shouldn't have made love to me then," she said crossly.

"Why not? Didn't you want to?" he asked, his voice cold. She leaped from the bed and went to the porthole and glared out of it. He put on his trousers and went into the galley. When he'd finishing making bacon and eggs she appeared, wearing an old shirt of his and the bottom of her bathing suit. Her eyes were a hard blue, piercing, angry.

"You never did give a damn, really, did you?" she said accusingly.

"Drop it, Julie," he answered. "Don't end it this way. You wouldn't understand, and I'm not explaining so leave it where it is."

"No, you don't understand," she said, and suddenly her voice was soft, hurt. "I don't have anything now," she went on. "Nothing and nobody. Not Pops, probably not even the house."

"You've got a lot, Julie," he said. "You've got yourself. You've got you. You're a beautiful girl. You're young and healthy. You've got the whole world to pick from."

"I don't want the whole world. I want you, Logan," she sobbed. Of all her shifting, changing moods this was her most powerful, the lost waif, the homeless stray. "Take the diamonds back but let me stay," she sobbed. "Please, Logan."

Logan's lips were grim. He felt the anger inside him bubbling to the surface. She'd done it to him once before. She wouldn't do it again. He'd sampled her sudden shifts. And he'd sampled her duplicity. He had a long memory.

"We made a deal," he said. "That's it."

He turned away from her. Damn but she was a deadly combination, throbbing beauty and helpless appeal. He took a cup and poured himself some coffee. He had just put it to his lips when he heard her voice, hard now, cold and angry.

"All right, I want the diamonds, Logan," he heard her say. "Give them to me."

He glanced at her and saw the heavy barrel of his Colt Python pointing at his stomach. It didn't move. It didn't waver or shake or wander. She held it steady as a rock. His lips tightened. She'd taken it from his cabin after he'd gone to the galley.

"This won't work, either, Julie," he said, looking deeply into her eyes. He saw only angry impatience.

"It'll work," she said grimly. "First in Mexico, then maybe South America. Like you said, diamonds don't rot, and they do bring a nice piece of change on the open market."

She motioned with the Colt. "Get them," she said. She carefully kept her distance from him. He turned and went into the cabin and took the little sack out of the draw. "Throw them to me," she said. He threw them.

"You don't know what you want to be, do you?" he said to her.

"Maybe not," she shot back. "But I don't want to be poor, and I don't want to be alone. These will help take care of both those things."

"No they won't, Julie," Logan said. "What about the old man? Will this do right by him?"

"You leave him out of this, damn you," she shouted back at him, but he knew he'd drawn blood.

"Start the engines," she commanded. "Get this tub as close to shore as it'll go. Bring it in until it scrapes bottom. Make it fast, Logan. I've got places to go."

Logan's smile was grim, with a ruefulness in it she ignored. It was an error. It was never wise to ignore anything Logan did. He started the *Urchin's* powerful engines and slowly moved the boat toward the shore. He got in pretty close before he felt the soft scrape of a sandy bottom against the hull. He switched off the engines and looked down at the water. It was clear and he could see bottom, not more than four and a half feet down. He walked out of the pilot-house onto the deck. Julie was amidships, one foot on the gunwale, still holding the Colt on him. She had the little sack in her other hand.

"Don't try coming after me, Logan," she warned him. "I'll use this thing."

"I won't," he said quietly. She lifted herself onto the gunwale and jumped overboard. She hit the water and got her footing on the bottom to wade onto the beach. She turned at the edge of the water to look at him. Logan walked into the pilot-house, put the boat's engines in reverse and slowly pulled her from the soft, sandy bottom. He swung the *Urchin* around slowly, and he was stern to the beach when he heard her cry out.

"Logan!" she screamed as it was all there in that one word, fury, astonishment, towering disappointment. He looked back at her. She was standing there, the little sack open, holding the fifteen little pebbles he had put into it in her hand. He waved a hand to her as he started to sail away.

"Logan! Come back, Logan," she called. "Logan, I'm sorry. Please come back."

Her voice carried the bitter disappointment and the real fear that was in her. He heard her sob. "I'm sorry, Logan," she cried. "Please, wait. Please, Logan."

It wasn't an act, that lost waif part of her, no more than the throbbing sexuality was an act. It was there, a part of her, and it came across the water to him. He wondered if the house were still standing. And he wondered how alone she really would be. She wasn't one of the crowd, he knew. She never had been. Her world had fallen in on her, had died with the old man on the beach. Damn it, he swore to himself. She could get to you.

"Logan, please," her cry followed after him and then there was a long moment of silence. He was going to look back when she called out again.

"You bastard, Logan," she called. "You sonofabitch! Don't you ever come back, you hear me?"

Logan grinned, and he shoved the *Urchin's* throttle to full speed. He was still grinning as he roared toward the mouth of the cove. She'd make it. Whenever it got too bad the hellcat would take over. He looked back as he went through the narrow entranceway to the cove. She was striding along the beach, walking toward Bayville and Kingdom Point, swinging the little sack vigorously as she went. He put his head back and laughed as he headed out to sea. When he had changed course for Bayville he put on the automatic pilot and went into the galley. Taking down a tin can, he poured the diamonds into his hand and looked at them. They did owe him something. They owed something to the spirit of hope and goodness. An old man had been killed because of them. He took two and put them aside. The rest he'd turn over to the police with a note, unsigned. They'd take it from there and work backwards to piece it all together. But he put the two he'd laid aside into a drawer of the little wall desk in the cabin. Then he took out a piece of notepaper and began to write on it.

Dear Sister Mary Angela,

A separate little package is being mailed to you. It will contain two small objects you can convert into dollars, about fifteen hundred dollars I'd guess. Believe it or not, they were found on a beach. It's time they did someone some good. With everlasting gratitude for that which you did for me.

As always,
Logan

He put the note into an envelope and placed it in the pocket of his jacket. He'd mail that in Bayville, along with the little package. His eyes held both a cold fire and a sadness. The old man on the beach was dead and the world cared nothing about it. But maybe something good had been salvaged out of it, the life of a child somewhere else, a new hope for someone without medicine. But he wondered if the day would come when he wouldn't always have to salvage good out of the debris of life. Maybe it would, sometime. Meanwhile, he steered his own course, and searched for that moment, the something that would make it all meaningful again. And he paused to enjoy all the way stations of pleasure. That's what kept him going. That and the search.

THE END